Mum in Waiting

MAUREEN CHILD

SILHOUETTE
DESIRE

Silhouette, Silhouette Desire and Colophon are registered trademarks of Harlequin Books S.A., used under licence.

First published in Great Britain 2000
Large Print edition 2002
Silhouette Books Limited,
Eton House, 18-24 Paradise Road,
Richmond, Surrey TW9 1SR

© Maureen Child 1999

ISBN 0 373 04798 3

Set in Times Roman 16¾ on 18½ pt.
36-0802-44935

Printed and bound in Great Britain
by Antony Rowe Ltd, Chippenham, Wiltshire

MAUREEN CHILD

was born and raised in Southern California, and is the only person she knows who longs for an occasional change of season. She is delighted to be writing for Silhouette® and is especially excited to be a part of the Desire™ line.

An avid reader, Maureen looks forward to those rare rainy California days when she can curl up and sink into a good book. Or two. When she isn't busy writing, she and her husband of twenty-five years like to travel, leaving their two grown-up children in charge of the neurotic golden retriever who is the *real* head of the household. Maureen is also an award-winning historical writer under the names Kathleen Kane and Ann Carberry.

To the owners and operators of the Crescent Beach Motel in Crescent City, California. You have the most beautiful spot on Highway 101... thanks for sharing it with us.

And to the City of Newport, Oregon. Your scenery is as gorgeous as your citizens are warm and friendly.

One

———

"I hate reunions," Tracy Hall muttered into the telephone receiver. This had seemed like such a good idea. Go home to Oregon. Attend a joint reunion for the last forty graduating classes of their tiny high school.

Now that her departure date had arrived, though, Tracy was seriously reconsidering the plan she'd thought brilliant a few weeks ago and that now seemed idiotic.

Still grumbling, she plopped down hard on top of her suitcase. She had enough clothes stuffed into the bag for a trip around the world. And that wasn't even counting her brand-new garment bag that literally bulged with dresses, high heels and purses or her cosmetic bag that now held several tons of makeup and lotions.

From her precarious seat, she leaned forward and clicked the latches shut, one after the other, with a sigh of triumph. The suitcase groaned a little as she scooted off, but she ignored it.

A flutter of nerves rose up and twisted in the pit of her stomach. What if this didn't work? What if someone found out what she was doing? Just imagining the gales of laughter made her groan and grit her teeth.

"Why am I doing this again?" she wondered aloud.

"Because it'll be fun," the voice on the phone told her.

"Yeah," Tracy said, unconvinced. "So far, it's a blast." The preparation alone for this little trip into her past had just about worn her out. And that didn't even take into account

The Plan. She even thought of it in capital letters.

"Honestly, Tracy," her sister Meg said in the drill sergeant tone she used on her children, "you might *try* for a little enthusiasm."

Well, she had been enthusiastic. A few weeks ago. When this silly idea of hers had first occurred to her. Now that she was actually having to go through with it, though, the notion had lost a little of its sparkle.

She looked into the mirror directly opposite her. Since the image was out of focus, she closed her left eye. She'd been in the middle of putting in her new contacts when Meg called, so she was now only half-blind.

The woman staring back at her from the glass looked quietly elegant, professional, confident—if you ignored the squint. Which just went to prove how deceiving appearances are. Because beneath the flashy new veneer, she was the same old Tracy Hall. The class nerd. The outcast. Ugly duckling to her older sister Meg's swan.

So, she'd never be a cover girl. She'd

learned to live with that. But, she told herself, even ugly ducklings grow up. And become, if not gorgeous swans, at least not-too-bad ducks.

"Tracy?" Meg said loudly. "You still there?"

"Yeah, I'm here," she said, smiling at the growing noise from Meg's end of the phone. "What's going on?"

"Just the usual," her sister said with a rueful laugh, then, half covering the mouthpiece, yelled, "Tony! Don't jump from the top of the stairs. You'll break your neck!"

"Is he a good old-fashioned super hero?" Tracy asked, picturing her youngest nephew in his latest death-defying feat.

"You are way out of the loop, little sister," Meg replied. "They're passé. We're into Power Rangers and Hercules."

A twinge of regret skittered through Tracy. She was out of the loop and she knew it. At twenty-eight, she was no closer to having children of her own than she had been at thirteen. The only thing about her situation that *had* changed was the fact that she'd finally come to grips with the idea that she would probably never have the family she used to dream about.

Working out of your home, alone, was not conducive to meeting single men.

"I'd better go," Meg said with a tired sigh. "Jenny's got her Xena, Warrior Princess costume on and she's challenging Hercules to a fight to the death."

Tracy smiled. She might not ever get to be a mom, but she loved every minute of being an aunt. And reunion or not, she was looking forward to spending a few days with all four of her nieces and nephews. "Where are Becky and David?" she asked, wondering about Meg's two oldest kids.

"Probably selling tickets to the fight," her sister said. "Half the neighborhood's arriving as we speak."

A car horn caught her attention and Tracy walked to the nearest window. "Speaking of arriving," she muttered as she watched the black Range Rover pull into her driveway. "Rick's here."

She squinted against the sun's glare and closed her left eye, but still couldn't see the driver. As she stared, a tall, shapeless blob of shadows emerged from the car, closed the door and locked it.

"How does he look?" Meg demanded.

"Blurry."

"Put your glasses on." An exasperated sigh followed that direct order.

She kept her gaze locked on the blur and asked, "*Exactly* what did he say when you asked him to give me a ride?"

"He said, and I quote, 'Sure,' unquote," Meg said.

Mistake, Tracy told herself. Maybe *huge* mistake. "Y'know," she said aloud, "the mechanic insists my car is fine now. I probably wouldn't have any trouble driving myself."

"Uh-huh. And he's the same mechanic who *fixed* it the last time?"

"Well, yeah." Tracy frowned as the blurry

figure moved toward her condo. "But he's learned a lot since then."

"I should hope so," Meg muttered.

"Everybody has to work their way up in their profession. Jimmy's improving all the time." And Tracy would not try to explain to her sister why she couldn't desert the young mechanic for one who was more skilled. But she wasn't going to be the one to shatter Jimmy's confidence by abandoning his shop.

Still, she didn't exactly trust his abilities enough to drive home by herself, either.

"It's not too late to take a plane," Meg said, her voice teasing.

"Oh, no." Tracy shook her head. "Planes are heavier than air. They fall. And they fall from really high up." Nope. No way was she going to get into an airplane. "But I could take the train."

"Oh, for heaven's sake, Tracy," Meg said, impatience coloring her tone. "What's the big deal? Rick was driving up for the reunion anyway."

True. And since he was stationed at Camp

Pendleton, just twenty or so miles south of Tracy's house, she really was on his way north. Camp Pendleton. She'd been tempted once or twice over the last couple of years to drive down to the base and see Rick...just for old-time's sake. But she'd always talked herself out of it.

Accepting a ride from him today might feel a lot less awkward if she hadn't.

"I don't know," Tracy said and leaned forward, watching him, until her forehead hit the cold windowpane. "It just seems weird, that's all. I haven't seen him in more than ten years. What if we don't have anything to talk about? It's a long drive to Oregon."

Meg actually laughed at that one. "Since when do you have trouble talking?"

True. Since growing out of her gangly, adolescent years, Tracy had made up for lost time. Her father had often said that given enough time, Tracy could talk the ears right off a statue.

Of course, good-looking men still had the ability to make her tongue-tied and distinctly uncomfortable. Besides, this was *Rick*. She could almost feel her nerves gathering for a good old-fashioned anxiety attack. Instantly, old memories rose up in her brain and she almost cringed.

As if reading her mind, Meg added, "I'm sure he's forgotten all about your stalker tendencies."

"Stalker?" Tracy straightened up. "I never stalked him. "I...*watched* him. From a discreet distance."

"Yeah," Meg said on another laugh. "From behind every tree and bush on the block."

Remembering those long-ago days brought back echoing waves of teenage angst. How she had loved Rick Bennet. Her big sister's boyfriend.

From below, she heard a brisk series of knocks on the door. Releasing old memories, she jumped into action.

"Gotta go, Meg," Tracy said, ignoring her sister's yelp of protest. "See ya soon." She hung up and hurried to the bathroom. Rick would have to wait a minute or two. She wasn't going to meet him with only one lens in. If she was going to pull off this little plan of hers, she wanted to get it right from the beginning.

Flipping on the light, she picked up her other contact lens and tipped her head back. She'd been practicing using the damn things for a week now, and she was still uncomfortable sticking foreign objects into her eyes.

But she'd get better. She had to. Her thick glasses were a part of the old Tracy. And that girl was *not* going to the reunion.

"Done," she said to herself, and tried to stop the wild blinking of her left eye. Like a twitch, her eyelid jerked and fluttered as if it was catching on the lens, which it probably was.

The doorbell rang, clanging and bonging like the bells of Big Ben. Apparently, he'd given up on knocking.

"Oh, swell," she said and clamped one hand over her left eye. Rick was downstairs and she was going to meet him for the first time in years looking like a one-eyed pirate. No time to start over, though. She had to hurry down and let him in before he rang that stupid bell again.

The previous owners of her condo had obviously suffered from delusions of grandeur, installing a doorbell with tones that rivaled a church organ. And, since moving in six months ago, she hadn't had time to have it replaced.

She'd been too busy establishing her at-home business and then getting herself in shape for what promised to be a very interesting high school reunion. With any luck.

Half stumbling down the stairs, Tracy muttered curses as behind her hand, her eyeball watered and itched. She ached to rub it but was afraid she'd send that new lens into what was left of her brain.

The bell pealed again and the reverberations had hardly faded away before she opened the door and came face-to-face with a big part of her past.

He still looked blurry.

But her memory filled in the blanks and her stomach did a quick series of twists and flips. Just like the old days.

Oh, this was going to be a *long* road trip.

"Tracy?"

"Hi," she said and winced at the squeaking sound coming out of her mouth instead of her normal voice. Lord, *his* voice still had the power to rumble along her spine with mind-numbing speed. Tracy swallowed hard to dislodge the sudden lump in her throat, but didn't try to speak again just yet. Instead, she stepped back and waved him inside with her free hand as she tried to remind herself she was not fourteen anymore. That shy, gawky teenager had grown into a widely sought-after computer wizard.

So why, she wondered, could she almost feel the tin wires of her braces digging into her lips? "Come on in," she finally managed to say.

Rick Bennet had not been looking forward to this. He'd only agreed to give Tracy a ride as a favor to Meg, his high-school girlfriend.

But the Tracy he remembered was nothing like the woman standing in front of him now.

In his memory, she was a shy, slightly overweight, fingernail-chewing, ponytail-wearing irritant. The younger sister he'd had to put up with every time he'd arrived at the Hall house to see Meg.

The girl who used to walk past his parents' house a dozen times a day. The girl who had trailed after him like a smaller shadow.

Obviously though, times—and Tracy—had changed.

He experienced a quick, hot jab of pure male admiration. It had been a long time since a woman had so instantly affected him. A flash of desire spurted into life as his gaze swept over her.

Her short blond hair was a fluffy tousle of curls that made him want to reach out and touch them, to test their softness against his skin. She wore a simple yellow blouse tucked into a calf-length, filmy looking summer skirt and small strappy sandals on her dainty feet. Pale pink nail polish decorated her toes, and with surprise he noted her tiny silver toe ring. Long, abstract silver drops hung from her earlobes, glinting in the afternoon sunlight. A honey-golden tan accentuated her blond hair and blue eyes, making her look like a magazine ad for youthful living in Southern California.

She made his mouth water. And though his brain had a hard time believing this desirable creature was really Tracy Hall...his body didn't care.

"Wow," he muttered. "You look great," he said, yet noted the hand she kept clamped over one eye and the fact that she was squinting with her other eye.

"Yeah," she grumbled just under her breath. "For a one-eyed pirate princess."

"Something wrong?"

"No," she said, as he stepped past her into the entry hall. "It's just these darn contacts."

Well, that explained the absence of the thick, wire-rimmed glasses he'd recalled. But what explained the rest of her transformation? he wondered silently. Like a butterfly from a little caterpillar, Tracy Hall had become a stunner.

His gaze followed her as she shut the door and turned to face him.

"Look," she said, keeping her hand firmly clasped over her eye. "Why don't you go into the living room while I run upstairs and see if I can get this darn thing out without blinding myself?"

Grabbing a fistful of skirt, she hiked the hem up to her knees and raced up the steps leading to the second story. Rick watched her, idly admiring the flash of her legs and the sweet curve of her behind.

That thought caught him up short. *Tracy's* behind? Little Tracy? Bookworm and math whiz? "Whoa," he told himself and rubbed the back of his neck. Shaking his head at this unexpected development, Rick turned and walked toward the doorway opening into the living room.

Another surprise.

He didn't know why, but he hadn't imagined Tracy living in such quiet elegance. Twin white sofas, their stark surfaces brightened with boldly colored throw pillows, sat facing each other. A low-slung coffee table that looked like a polished redwood stump lay between them and held a scattering of magazines neatly fanned out on its surface. A couple of overstuffed chairs, small decorator tables and reading lamps made up the rest of the furniture in the large, airy room. Two of the four walls were completely covered by bookcases. Another wall boasted floor-to-ceiling windows with a view of the ocean in the distance. On the last wall was a fireplace with a basket of wood sitting on its hearth. The wide plank floors gleamed in the splash of sunlight streaming through the uncurtained windows.

Just one surprise after another. When he had agreed to give Tracy a ride home to Oregon, he'd somehow expected to find her in a small apartment, locked away from the world. Stupid, he supposed, to assume that a grown woman would be much the same as she had been at fourteen. Just because she had spent most of her time then hidden behind the pages of a book didn't mean the same would hold true now.

He couldn't help wondering if her personality had changed as thoroughly as her appearance.

Upstairs, Tracy raced into her bedroom, clipped her hip on the edge of her dresser and ran into the bathroom, wincing at the low throb of pain. Another bruise soon, she thought. Honestly, she was black and blue enough to convince anyone that she was being abused regularly.

But in her own defense, she wasn't really clumsy. She was simply always rushing, thinking ahead to what her next move would be to the extent that she didn't pay attention to what she was doing at the moment.

And right now, she was thinking about the next three days spent in a car—and motels— with Rick Bennet.

Setting both palms down flat on the edge of the sink, she leaned forward and dragged several deep breaths into lungs that felt starved for air. "Jeeezzz, why'd he have to be so good looking *still?* Why couldn't he have developed a hunch back, adult acne and bad teeth?"

The butterflies in her stomach had butterflies of their own. One look at him and her heartbeat had quickened until she wouldn't have been surprised to see it fly right out of her chest.

Just imagine what her reaction might have been if he'd arrived wearing his Marine uniform. Ooohh…the thought of that had her toes curling tightly into her new sandals.

What was it about Rick Bennet that got to her? Even as a kid, Tracy had watched his every move and daydreamed about him breaking up with her sister, Meg, in favor of her. She'd gone to sleep every night kissing a pillow, pretending it was him. She'd filled dozens of diaries detailing every word he ever said to her, which wasn't difficult since most of their conversations had been limited to… "Hi, Rick," from her and "Hey kid, where's Meg?" from him.

Not much, true, but enough to warm every corner of a nerdy fourteen-year-old girl's heart.

And now…he had actually paid her a compliment. Obviously, the professional makeover she'd sprung for had been worth every penny.

She lifted her head, stared into the mirror and groaned. "Oh, yeah. You're a real beauty, you are."

Prying open her eyelid, she fumbled for a minute or two, then finally managed to adjust the annoying contact lens.

Studying her reflection, she had to wonder if this was worth all the trouble. Not just the contacts. She'd eventually get used to them. No, she was beginning to doubt the wisdom of her whole plan.

But reunions didn't come along every day. And heck, she'd heard people talking about going back to their old schools and lying like crazy about their grand achievements in life. And it wasn't as though she was going home pretending to be the president of the United States or something.

She flipped off the light switch and walked into the bedroom. Sunlight filtered through the sky-blue blinds and lay in golden slats across her quilt-covered bed. Almost like sunshine sliding through prison bars. Except that they were lying horizontally instead of vertically and prisons probably didn't have such homey touches as quilts and feather pillows. And besides, they didn't put you in jail for lying, did they?

A guilty conscience nudged her again.

"Oh, perfect," she mumbled, striding toward the bed to pick up her bags. "It's a good thing you didn't become a criminal," she said aloud. "Or a spy. You just don't have the stomach for it."

Who was she trying to kid? It wasn't the thought of living a lie for the reunion that had her so tied up in knots. It was seeing Rick again. It was feeling those old feelings again. It was realizing that some things, no matter how many years had passed, didn't change.

Slinging her garment bag over one shoulder, she staggered under its weight, groaned, then lifted the metal bar on her suitcase and set its tiny back wheels on the pine floor. Grabbing up her cosmetic case, she headed for the doorway with slow, plodding steps.

Like a man headed up the stairs of a gallows. "Oh, get a grip, Tracy," she told herself. Honestly, if she was going to spend the next week or two sweating over every tiny white lie—excuse me, *exaggeration*—she'd never make it.

And for heaven's sake, she'd better get over the flutter of nerves that attacked whenever she was within an arm's reach of Rick. He was doing a favor for her sister. Just being friendly. He wasn't there as her date. Or her lover.

Ooohh. That thought sent a tingling sensation to every part of her body. Slowly, deliberately, she pulled in a long, deep breath, hoping to stabilize her nervous system.

When she was in control again, she lifted her chin and said aloud, "You can do this, y'know. It's just a few days alone with him. Then you won't see him for another ten years or so. How hard can it be?''

Something told her that last sentence would go down in her private journal as the equivalent of ''famous last words.''

Two

Freeway miles flew past.

In just a few hours, they were out of the Los Angeles area's crush of cars and speeding along a highway edged on either side by acres of farm country. Orange and apple groves blended into small, tidy vineyards and those into pistachio orchards. The sky seemed bluer, the sun warmer and the wind cleaner.

Tracy stared out the window at the passing scenery, noting the ancient California oaks—now protected by the state—dotting the rolling hillsides. Occasional farm houses added

touches of color to the rain-freshened green-
ery. The farther they traveled from home and
the work that awaited her return, the more
Tracy relaxed into the plush seat cushion.

This wasn't so bad, she told herself. Actually, it had been a pretty nice trip so far. She
hadn't stumbled over a conversation once, and
she was almost used to Rick being in such
close proximity to her.

Of course, she'd be in way better shape if
he weren't.

She slid a sidelong glance in his direction.
Both hands on the wheel, he kept his gaze
locked on the road in front of him. But, even
in profile, his good looks were enough to fuel
a dozen or more very interesting fantasies in
far less susceptible women than she.

His light brown hair was cut militarily
short, yet retained just enough length to let her
see traces of what used to be soft waves. He
wore a pair of silver-framed aviator-style sunglasses that hid his deep emerald-green eyes.
At six foot one, he was much taller than she,
even sitting down, and his dark blue polo

shirt, open at the collar, stretched across a broad chest that proved he had more than a passing acquaintance with weight lifting.

Her gaze slid down briefly, noting his faded blue jeans and the slip-on deck shoes he wore. Yep. Gorgeous. She bit back a groan and deliberately turned her gaze back to the road ahead of them.

"Inspection over?" he inquired politely.

"Excuse me?" she glanced at him, feigning confusion.

"Did I pass?" He spared her a quick, amused look.

Obviously, he wasn't going to buy her innocent act.

"Saw that, huh?" No point in denying what he'd clearly noticed.

"Subtlety was never your strong suit, Tracy," he said and one corner of his mouth quirked into a half smile.

"Still not," she admitted. Shifting in her seat, she gave him her full attention. "Though I rarely hide behind trees these days."

His smile deepened.

"Anyway, I was just noticing that you really haven't changed much over the years." An understatement somewhere along the lines of "Gee, the Empire State Building's a little tall."

"You sure have," he countered and shot another half glance her way. "You look great."

"Thanks," she said. "I think."

He laughed shortly. "Okay, that didn't quite sound the way I meant it to."

"It's all right. I know what you meant." A gust of air rushed through her open window, pushing her hair into her eyes. She swept it back with an impatient gesture.

She should be pleased, she thought. Wasn't he seeing her exactly the way she wanted all of the people back home to see her? Changed? Grown up? Beautiful? So why did it irritate her that Rick Bennet was noticing the very image she'd worked so hard to portray?

Maybe because there was a part of her that wanted a man to be attracted to the real Tracy? She couldn't help wondering what it might have felt like to have Rick look at her as she usually was, in jeans and T-shirt, and still think she was beautiful.

"So," he asked, turning down the volume on the car radio, "how come you're making the trip home?"

"Probably for the same reasons as you," she said. "To see the family. Visit. Stroll through the school and see if it's as hideous as I remember it."

"Hideous?" he repeated. "I always thought you liked school."

"Why?" she asked. "Because I studied all the time, got good grades?"

"Well," he said with a shrug. "Yeah."

A natural assumption, she supposed. It would never have occurred to him that she'd spent all of her time studying because she was too shy to make friends and too awkward to attract boys. School was the one and only place where Tracy shone, which had pleased her proud parents no end, but had also contributed to her nerd reputation. Of course, her doom was sealed when she skipped a grade.

Not only was she younger than everyone else, but a geek, as well. Every time some teacher had held her up to the class as an example of what could be accomplished through actual study, the resentment level at Juneport High had escalated.

Her one real friend had been her sister, Meg, which had only made Tracy's lusting after Rick even more awful.

"Talked to my mom last week," he was saying, and Tracy steered her attention back to the here and now. "She tells me Meg's pregnant again."

"Yep." Swiftly, stirrings of both excitement and envy rippled through Tracy. Deliberately, she pushed the latter into a dark corner of her heart, hoping it would stay there.

But oh, how she would have loved to be somebody's mother.

"How many does that make?"

"This is her fifth," Tracy said, smiling at the idea of another new baby to cuddle. The warm, solid weight of a tiny human being cradled against her was the sweetest feeling she could imagine. She'd have to take a couple of weeks vacation when the newest niece or nephew arrived, just so she could indulge her status of favored aunt—and, work out some of her own frustrated baby fever pangs.

"Five kids!" Rick shook his head and whistled to himself, low and long.

"What's wrong with that?" she demanded, instantly on the defensive.

"Whoa, Aunt Tracy," he said, taking one hand from the wheel long enough to hold it up in mock surrender. "I only meant it's hard to imagine Meg—or John, for that matter— having five kids."

"Oh." Her protective instincts subsiding just a bit, Tracy said, "Okay. It's just that a lot of people make a big deal out of how many kids she has. And I don't figure it's anybody's business but Meg and John's. Besides, who says the nuclear family has to be limited to 2.5 children?"

He chuckled and shook his head. "Not me. I don't see the appeal in having kids, but like you said, that's their business."

"Good, because she'll probably make sure you get to meet the whole brood."

Rick's eyes widened at the thought until he looked like a deer caught in headlights. Apparently, the very idea of being surrounded by kids was enough to turn the big bad Marine pale as a ghost. Still the confirmed bachelor then, she thought with a wistful sigh.

Not that she would ever have had a chance with him anyway. But she wanted a man who wanted the same things she did. Home. Family. A big, sloppy dog.

"You're excited about seeing the kids, aren't you?"

"Is it that obvious?"

"Oh, yeah," he said and grinned at her. "Your face lit up and there was a distinct gleam in your eyes."

"I'm a very good aunt," she said.

He looked at her again, this time thoughtfully. "I'll bet you are."

Rick had the feeling that Tracy was pretty damn good at whatever she did. She'd always had a soft heart. And, he might remember her as being an annoyance, but he also remembered just how smart she was. With perfect clarity, he recalled how humiliated he'd been to have a fourteen-year-old girl tutor him in geometry. Of course, without her help, he might still be sitting in Mr. Molino's classroom, staring blankly at the chalkboard as though trying to decipher ancient hieroglyphs.

Back then, all he'd wanted to do was play football and spend every other spare minute with Meg. She had been his first real love and he'd been sure that they would be together for the rest of their lives.

He pulled in a deep breath and let himself remember the night that particular dream had died.

It was the night after high school graduation. They were supposed to meet at the gym, then drive to Reno and get married. Stupid, he told himself now. But at the time, it had all seemed so romantic. So adult. Suitcase packed, graduation money in his pocket, he'd driven to the gym and parked in the shadow-filled lot to wait for her. Hours passed, and at first he'd assumed she was having trouble getting away. Then later, he'd found other, more complex excuses for her. At last, he fell asleep only to wake up as dawn filtered through the darkness. He was still alone.

Naturally, he'd driven straight to Meg's. Convinced that only illness or a broken bone could have kept her from their rendezvous, he'd been surprised when she'd hustled out of the quiet house in her bathrobe to meet him on the lawn.

All these years later, he could still hear her voice, tinged with regret.

"I'm sorry, Rick. But I just couldn't go through with it."

"But why?" he'd demanded, and made a grab for her, which she quickly sidestepped.

"I can't explain it, really," she said as a single tear sneaked from the corner of her eye. "But it just doesn't feel right."

"Right? Of course it's right," he argued. "We love each other."

Meg shook her head. "I can't marry you. Not now. Not like this."

"When, then?" he asked, following her as she backed up toward her house.

"Rick, please understand," she said in a strained whisper. "I don't...I can't..." She shook her head, turned around and bolted for the safety of her house.

Left alone in the dawn silence, Rick had taken what was left of his eighteen-year-old heart, wrapped it up in his battered pride and gone home himself. The next day, he'd left early for college, spending the summer working as far away from Juneport, Oregon, as possible.

Meg wrote to him, months later, apologizing again before informing him that she was now engaged to marry his best friend, John Bingham.

By then though, he'd already come to believe that Meg had done them both a favor by backing out of their plans. Love's wounds are deep, but when you're young, they heal fairly quickly.

Once out of college, Rick had entered the Marines as an officer. He liked his job. His life. And every once in a while, he silently thanked Meg for having been smarter than he was so long ago.

Besides. *Five* kids? No matter what dear Aunt Tracy thought, the idea of five kids was enough to give him cold chills. Of course, since he was in no hurry to get married, that wasn't something he had to worry about.

He'd managed to avoid any permanent entanglements for thirty-two years. Not that he had anything against marriage as a general rule. Rick squirmed uncomfortably in his seat. He came from a long line of Happily Ever After marriages. Not one couple on either side of his family had ever been divorced, and he had no intention of being the first.

God knew, he'd seen first hand just how tough military life was on spouses. Relationships crumbled with sad regularity. Rick wasn't about to get married when he knew damn well that he couldn't give a wife the kind of attention and devotion she had a right to expect.

He was a Marine, first and foremost. And

not many women could understand, let alone accept that.

"So," Tracy asked, and her voice brought him out of his reveries, "what are your brothers up to? Have they made you an uncle yet?"

Rick laughed at the idea. "Heck, no. There's not a woman alive who'd be willing to put up with either one of them."

"Oh, very nice," she said, a soft smile on her face.

Had she always had that tiny dimple? he wondered.

"They're in the Marines too, aren't they?" she asked.

He nodded. "Andy's a lieutenant and Jeff is a gunnery sergeant. They'll both be home for the reunion."

"And you're looking forward to seeing them."

"Oh, yeah." The Bennet family hadn't all been together in one place in years. "It's been way too long."

"Imagine. All three of you becoming Marines."

"Not so hard to figure with a retired sergeant major for a father."

"No, I guess not." She laughed, and Rick smiled at the soft, almost musical sound of it. Something inside him tightened as he realized he was really enjoying himself.

With Tracy.

Scowling, he told himself to keep his mind on his driving and off the idle fantasies beginning to swirl through his brain.

"Do you remember," she asked next, "when Andy swiped your bike, left it on the beach and it went out on the tide?"

Grateful for the distraction, he asked, "Remember it?" Shaking his head, he said, "The guy still owes me thirty-five dollars for that bike. I delivered newspapers for months to earn the money to buy it."

"Poor baby," she cooed.

"No sympathy from you, apparently."

"Of course not," she said on a laugh. "That's one of my best memories. Andy gave me a ride on the handlebars that day. I was with him when the bike went for its long last swim.''

''You're kidding!'' He glanced at her, then looked back at the road.

''Would I kid about a thing like that?'' She shook her head and laughed at the memory. ''We swam out into the ocean, chasing that darn bike, but apparently King Neptune needed some transportation, because it disappeared real quick.''

He tried to imagine the young, hopelessly awkward Tracy, swimming out to sea after a bike, but looking at the woman beside him made it darn near impossible. ''He never said anything to me about that.''

She lifted her chin, crossed her heart with her fingertips, then held up the regulation three-fingered salute. ''Partners in crime do not squeal on each other.''

''Until now?'' he asked.

Tracy nodded. ''I think the statute of limitations has about run out.''

''That's what you think, Spot,'' he said, unconsciously using the nickname he'd christened her with one long ago summer. ''I'll be settling up with each of you now. Your share comes to seventeen fifty.''

Tracy didn't say anything for a long minute.

''What's wrong?'' he asked. ''Going to refuse to pay up?''

She still didn't speak. He glanced at her and noted the wide, surprised look in her eyes. ''You called me Spot.''

''So I did,'' he said on a chuckle. Strange. Where had that come from? He hadn't thought of that nickname in years. But he certainly remembered the reason behind it. Every summer, Tracy's freckles had dotted her cheeks and nose as if someone had splattered her with soft peach paint. And, as he recalled, she wasn't very fond of his making fun of that fact. ''Huh.'' He changed lanes and spared her another look. ''Sorry, don't know why that popped out.''

''Oh, don't be sorry,'' she said and reached out to place one hand on his arm.

Rick's gaze dropped briefly to her long, slender fingers against his tanned forearm.

Hot, jagged bolts of electricity seemed to hum from her touch, reverberating deep inside him. Mouth dry, he told himself it was simply a normal male reaction to a pretty woman. But it was more than that and he knew it. She pulled her hand away too quickly for his tastes. But even after their connection had been broken, the echo of that surprising sizzle of heat lingered.

He rolled his window down, hoping the cool outside air would work on the sexual heat barbecuing him from the inside out.

"God, it's been years since I've even thought of that name," she whispered, half to herself.

"I don't know what made me think of it," he admitted. But being with her like this...memories filled the car like the scent of childhood summers.

He shifted in his seat again. What he was feeling at the moment had nothing whatever to do with the Tracy he remembered from years ago.

"I never told you," she said, her voice low

and thoughtful, "how much that nickname meant to me."

"What?" He steered the car into the far right lane. Less traffic meant he could shoot her another look. Her blue eyes looked misty, shimmering. And entirely too beautiful. "As I remember it, you were less than happy with me at the time."

"Oh, sure, I acted all insulted," Tracy said. "It was awful the way I used to freckle up after a couple of hours in the sun. Meg always got such a great tan and I looked, well, dreadful."

"Apparently, you've grown out of that," he pointed out, noticing again her pale golden tan.

"Not completely," she admitted. "It's just that the freckles don't pop out on my face anymore."

Instantly, Rick imagined seeing those mysteriously hidden freckles for himself. His body quickened and he bit back a groan of discomfort. Hell, who would have guessed that little

Tracy Hall could set his hormones in an uproar?

"But when you called me Spot..."

"Not very nice," he said in his own defense, "but I was a kid."

"I loved it."

He slowed down to match the pace of the produce truck ahead of them. "You did?"

"Oh, yes." She shoved her fingers through her hair, raking the curls back from her face and exposing the long elegant line of her throat. Those silver earrings twinkled in the sunlight. "Don't you see?" she asked. "For me, it was the first time you ever really noticed me."

He was noticing her plenty right now, but she appeared to be unaware of it.

"Oh," he said, "I noticed. Hard not to when you were walking your dog back and forth in front of the house every half hour."

She dipped her head and looked up at him, a smile curving lips that looked full and ripe and totally delicious.

"Again with the not subtle," she said,

chuckling. "When your mother made you stop calling me Spot, I thought my heart would break. My misery took up three whole pages in my diary."

He forced a rueful laugh from a too tight throat. "I wish you'd told me that. Could have saved me a week's grounding."

"Hey," she said, echoing his earlier excuse, "I was a kid."

Not anymore, he wanted to say, but somehow managed not to. Good God, he hadn't felt like this since he was a kid himself. His palms were sweating, his heartbeat thundered in his ears and he had to wonder if there was some sort of celestial irony in all of this.

Ten, fifteen years ago, he'd been the unwilling object of Tracy's desire—at least for a little while. Now, it seemed the tables had been neatly turned.

"Where are we going?" she asked as he steered the car into the exit lane.

"We need gas," he explained. "Might as well get something to eat while we're at it."

Plus, he needed to get out of the car and move around. Try to walk while he still could.

It was only late afternoon, and they could drive several more hours before stopping for the night. At that thought, he gave a heartfelt, though silent, groan. A motel. With Tracy.

Man. He hoped somebody somewhere was getting a good laugh out of this.

"Okay," she said, "and for our first night on the road, dinner's my treat."

He stopped at the end of the exit and gave her a smile he hoped didn't look forced. "At least seventeen fifty's worth."

"Deal."

Three

—

The coffee shop was crowded, indicating to two hungry travellers that the food was better than the decor. As she surveyed the room with wide eyes, Tracy desperately hoped so.

Dark wood paneling covered the walls and garishly colored baskets, containing long, trailing arms of plastic ivy, hung from the ceiling. Improbably colored sombreros were tacked to the walls and wagon-wheel chandeliers studded with candle-watt bulbs kept the place as dark as a cave.

But the waitress was friendly and took their

order quickly. As she moved off to the kitchen, Tracy took the opportunity to—all right—*stare* at Rick.

Even after several hours in his company, she hadn't looked her fill of that face. Strong jaw, sharp, straight nose, piercingly green eyes dotted with tiny gold flecks near the irises and a smile that had her insides screaming for mercy.

Amazing. She'd thought her feelings for him were safely buried years ago. Instead, here she sat, feeling that torch fan into flame again. The only difference between then and now was that the sensations were stronger, more raw. After all, she was grown up now. She had a lot more detailed—if still strictly theoretical—information to draw on for her fantasies.

Their waitress set glasses of iced tea down in front of them before disappearing back into the kitchen. Needing something to do with her hands, Tracy grabbed the oversize plastic container like a drowning man reaching for a life ring. She twirled the glass between her palms, making a chain of water rings along the Formica surface of the table.

She could only hope that the icy chill of the tea would help toward cooling off the blood rushing through her veins.

"So," he said.

"So," she said right back. Strange, they hadn't had any trouble talking in the car. Why so strained now? Because sitting opposite each other in a restaurant seemed too much like a date for comfort? Hah. *Her* on a date with Captain Rick Bennet? Not likely, despite what her imagination would like to think. Just to prove it to herself, she asked, "You said Andy and Jeff are still single. What about you?"

He took a sip of tea, set the glass down and said, "The same."

Tracy hadn't realized she was holding her breath until it slipped from her in a gust at his answer. A ripple of pleasure ran up her spine. As much as she knew she was indulging in a fool's paradise, she hadn't wanted to hear about his gorgeous girlfriend and/or live-in lover. Not to mention, God forbid, a fiancée.

"Mom's been making all of the traditional whining noises about grandchildren for the last few years," he said with a rueful laugh, "but at least for the foreseeable future, she's out of luck. I can't see either Andy or Jeff as daddies."

"What about you?"

"What about me?"

"You don't want kids?" she asked, then caught herself and added, "Oops. None of my business." Though the thought of seeing Rick's handsome features in a tinier version brought her all sorts of warm fuzzies.

He smiled and shook his head. "Traditionally speaking, you should be married to have kids and since I don't plan on doing that, I guess not."

She buried the quick flash of disappointment that shot through the pit of her stomach. For heaven's sake. Why should she be disappointed? What did she care if Rick wanted children or not? She didn't, she told herself,

although she *was* curious about why he was
so set against marriage.

Before she could think better of it, she
heard herself ask that question out loud. "As
long as I'm being nosey, why are you so
against marriage?"

"I'm not against the general idea of it," he
said. "Just as far as it concerns me."

"How come?" she asked.

"Lots of reasons," he answered, then
added glibly, "maybe I'm just too old."

To Tracy's admittedly biased eye, Rick had
aged just like good wine. He'd gotten
stronger, and more fully developed. At that
gooey thought, she felt a flush of heat steal up
her neck and bloom in her cheeks. Oh, this
was getting out of hand, she told herself.
Didn't she have enough to think about without
reigniting a nearly fifteen-year-old torch?

One more time, she tried for objectivity. A
casual conversation between two old—if not
friends—acquaintances.

"You're thirty-two Rick, not exactly Me-
thuselah."

He gave her a small smile. "Thanks, I think."

"So what's the real reason?" And why did she care?

Rick studied her for a long minute as if trying to decide whether or not to answer her question honestly. Finally, he said simply, "I already took one oath. To the Marines."

Now that surprised her. What would his being in the military have to do with taking a pledge against marriage?

"The Marines and families don't mix?"

"They can," he said, leaning back in the booth. "With the right kind of spouse."

"Intriguing," she said. "And what kind is the right kind?" If she was a little more interested in his answer than she pretended, he didn't have to know that.

"Oh," he tipped his head back and stared up at the ceiling. Frowning, he moved more to his right to avoid one of those skeletal plastic plant limbs. "Someone who doesn't mind moving every few years. Someone who can handle a partner's absences." To explain that one, he added, "Some outfits are deployed for six months at a time. And families don't go along." He took another long drink of tea. "You'd be surprised how many wives—and husbands for that matter—complain."

Seemed to her that if you married someone in the military, knowing what they did for a living, then you had no right to complain about the job description.

But what did she know? Though the idea of travelling all over the world—on a boat, not a plane—appealed to her, she could see how some women wouldn't exactly thrive on it.

"There's a trail of discarded wedding rings from here to Guam," Rick told her. "A military life will either make a marriage stronger than steel or shatter it completely."

"And you're not willing to risk it?"

"That's right," he said, giving that plant a look that should have melted its plastic roots. "I've sat and listened to too many of my friends when their marriages ended. It's not enough *they're* miserable...their children's lives have been ruined, too." He shook his head and stared directly into her eyes. "No, thanks. Not for me. I'm not going to be the first member of my family to get a divorce. And I'm sure as hell not going to make babies only to be forced into a custody suit somewhere down the line."

"Well," she said softly, "*there's* a positive attitude."

"I've seen too many negatives to make a positive."

"But lots of people do it," she pointed out.

"Sure. I have a few friends who've been married forever. But their wives put up with a lot." He took a deep breath and shook his head again as if trying to figure out just how and why the women did it. "The base housing alone is like a walk on the wild side. You're never even sure if you'll actually find a house on base available and when you do, more than likely it was built during the Second World War. Or the First. Model homes they're not."

Maybe she was just being a romantic, but did *where* you live count for more than *who* you lived with?

"Well," she said, "you grew up moving from base to base. Did you mind?"

"Not a bit," he admitted with a half smile. "To us, it was fun. Not always easy to make new friends, but we always had each other. New schools every few years. No time to really offend any one teacher before you were off to new territory."

"Until you landed in Juneport."

"True. When Dad left the Corps and settled down, it was hard to get used to at first." Bending forward, he leaned his elbows on the tabletop and cupped his drink between his palms. "Actually, staying put was harder on us than the constant moving around, for a while."

It might have been hard on him, she thought. But the day the Bennets had moved onto her block had been one of the highlights of her teenage life. Of course, she wasn't about to admit that out loud. It was bad enough that he had so many memories of her staring at him like an old, worshipful hound.

Instead, she said, "Yeah. Then you had

plenty of time to win the enmity of teachers. Mr. Molino for example?''

He shrugged exaggeratedly. ''Geometry. Still gives me nightmares.''

Strange how differently two people saw the same situation. She'd always been grateful for Rick's helplessness at math. Those tutoring sessions when she'd had him all to herself had been the stuff a fourteen-year-old's dreams were made of.

''Enough about me,'' he said suddenly, locking his gaze with hers. ''What's going on with you? Meg tells me you're some kind of superstar with computers.''

Had he asked Meg about her? she wondered, then told herself that was unlikely. Why would he have cared about the little twit he remembered?

''Not really,'' she said modestly. ''I design software and computer games.''

''And that's it?'' he asked. ''No way do you get off that easy. You had me spilling my guts. It's your turn now. Tell me about it. What exactly do you do?''

Wondering if he was really interested or just being polite, Tracy gave him a brief overview of what her daily job was like. When he asked a couple of pointed questions however, she warmed to her theme and probably ended up giving him way more information than he had counted on.

Ordinarily, there was nothing she liked better than to talk programs, games and all of the little intricacies of the computer world. But she noticed when his eyes started to glaze over and knew she'd done it again.

It never failed.

On the few occasions some living, breathing, male had actually asked her out, the conversation had turned to their work and Tracy's enthusiasm for hers generally had the effect of putting her date to sleep. First dates rarely rated a second, so Tracy had wound up being one of the last virgins known to exist in the modern world.

Which, at the ripe old age of twenty-eight, was an embarrassing secret she kept hidden with all the stealth of the Pentagon guarding nuclear information.

"Wow," he muttered when she finally wound down.

She gave herself a mental kick and remembered that on this trip, she wasn't going to be the computer nerd. On this trip, she was a new, interesting, *alluring* Tracy. If she could figure out how to pull it off.

"Sorry," she said, letting her gaze drop to her iced tea. "I tend to go a little overboard about my work."

"Yeah," he said with a nod. "Me, too. You'd be surprised how little women care about the inner workings of the military."

She smiled at him, and her embarrassment faded. He understood, she told herself. Understood what it was to love your work so much, you could talk about it for hours.

A moment of silence stretched out between them before Rick admitted, "Okay, I confess I didn't understand half of what you said. Math and its close relative, the computer, are still not my best things."

Nerd, nerd, nerd. She ought to just have the word tattooed on her forehead, so the unwary could walk a wide path around her.

"But I'm impressed as hell," he concluded, and her gaze snapped up to meet his.

"You are?" she asked. Unconvinced, she stared at him, looking for the telltale signs that he was simply being polite. Or worse yet, studying her with the fascination you might give a particularly talented lab rat.

But admiration shone in his eyes, and, unaccustomed to that reaction, Tracy didn't know what to say.

"So I guess you're some high-powered executive for some huge software place?"

"Nope." Not that she hadn't been offered positions just like the one he'd described. But as her mother used to say, she just didn't play well with other children. She'd never really been the nine-to-five sort of person. Rather, she tended to work in frantic spurts of creativity and industry that usually cropped up about 1:00 a.m. "I run my own business."

His eyebrows lifted high on his forehead.

"You always were smarter than anyone I knew," he said. "Your own boss, huh?"

Tracy felt an unexpected flush of pride steal over her. "Yes, and it's great. I get to work out of my house. No power suits for me."

His gaze dropped to take in her simple, summery outfit. "Who needs power suits when you look so good like that?"

Another flush swamped her. Not pride this time, but pure, unadulterated, feminine pleasure. Of course, if he ever got a look at her *real* work clothes—faded jeans and over-sized T-shirts—he'd probably change his tune. But then, for the week or so of the reunion festivities, she wasn't plain old Tracy Hall. She was the new and improved version—the woman put together by a professional shopper, a makeover artist and the best hairdresser she could find.

And judging from the look in Rick's eyes, the whole process had been worth every penny. If there was a small part of her that wished he would look at the *real* Tracy in the same way, she ignored it.

No point in torturing herself.

"Any boyfriends lurking in the shadows that I should be worried about?" he asked, shattering the very pleasant mood she'd had going.

"No." She stiffened slightly and forced herself to relax again.

"None?" He seemed surprised, then shot her a smile that sent wild flutters of appreciation rustling in her stomach. "You're sure no jealous lover's going to want to punch me in the nose for having you all to myself for three days?"

"Trust me," she told him and lifted her chin. "You're safe."

Shaking his head, he looked her over again slowly, as if trying to figure out why she was unattached.

"There just never seemed to be the time," she said, even though she knew darn well there'd been plenty of time, just no willing men flocking to her front door. At least, not more than once. Computer nerds weren't exactly at the top of the dating food chain.

"I'm amazed some man hasn't convinced you to take the time."

Amazed, huh? Well, that felt good, anyway.

"So we'll both be attending the reunion un- attached and available." He gave her a wry smile. "You do realize that we're going to be surrounded by former classmates clutching photo albums of children and spouses?"

"Oh, yeah." Actually, it was that realiza- tion that had given birth to the plan she'd for- mulated a few weeks ago.

"Outnumbered and trapped in a sea of fam- ily photos," he went on with an exaggerated shiver, "we'll have nothing to use as ammu- nition." Flashing her a quick wink, he sug- gested, "We should join forces, Tracy. Guard each other's backs. Protect our flanks."

Briefly, she enjoyed the thought of being a part of Rick Bennet's team. Being his partner in crime, so to speak. But, as interesting as that prospect sounded, Tracy had something wildly different in mind. She'd prepared for this, knowing that she didn't want to attend a reunion as "Poor Little Tracy, Still Manless After All These Years."

Just imagining the sympathetic yet knowing looks she would receive from the once popular kids was enough to strengthen her resolve. Darn it, she'd been second best through most of her life. She refused to go back home as single as she'd left it.

"Sorry, Rick," she told him with a slow shake of her head. "You're on your own."

"Thanks, pal." Surprise, and was that disappointment that flickered in his eyes? He leaned back in the booth, crossed his arms over that really terrific chest of his, locked his gaze on her and asked, "Whatever happened to camaraderie? Birds of a feather flocking together? Two peas in a pod?"

Her lips twitched as a smile fought for purchase. Attempting to match his light-hearted tone, she said, "Not that I have anything against joining you in a pod..."

His eyebrows lifted.

She cleared a suddenly tight throat and continued. "It's just that I've already taken care of the situation. At least as far as I'm concerned.''

Rick sat up abruptly and leaned forward, elbows braced on the table again. The overhead light cast soft shadows on his face. The plastic plant seemed to be reaching for him. He brushed it aside. "Okay, Ms. Genius, I'm intrigued. What's the plan?''

She opened her mouth to confess what would probably sound insane to him, but she didn't get the chance.

"Sorry it took so long, folks,'' the waitress announced as she hurried up to their table. Setting their dinner plates down in front of them, she gave them each a smile before asking if they wanted a tea refill.

"Sure, thanks,'' Rick said, "Tracy?''

"Yes, please,'' she said and nodded at the waitress. "Thanks, Bonnie.''

The tired-looking woman smiled at her. "No problem, honey.''

When she left to get the tea, Rick looked at Tracy. "How'd you know her name?''

"She's wearing a name tag," Tracy said with a shrug.

"Huh." Rick shook his head, then focused his gaze on her again as he picked up his knife and fork, preparing to dig into his halibut steak. "So, back to the subject at hand. What's the plan, Trace?"

She glanced at her breast of chicken plate and knew she'd never be able to force a bite down until she'd gotten this over with. And actually, she told herself, this was a very good thing. Sort of like a test case. Judging Rick's reaction might give her an idea of how all the folks back home would respond.

She nodded, took a deep breath, and reached into her purse. Tracy fumbled blindly in its depths. She felt his gaze on her which made her a little clumsier than usual. Mentally, she reminded herself that it was definitely time to clean out the purse again. It seemed the bigger her purses were, the more junk she managed to cram inside.

She squinted at the contents, but in the dim light, it took her several minutes to locate the little velvet box and then get it opened. Her fingertips moved across the sharp, cold edges of the stone nestled in the jeweler's box as she briefly rethought her brilliant plan. What if he laughed? Oh my, this suddenly felt so stupid. So childish. Her stomach twisted with nerves. But she'd come too far to quit now.

Setting her purse on the booth seat beside her, she slipped the tasteful but impressive ring she'd purchased last week on her finger beneath the cover of the table. Then, gritting her teeth and mentally preparing herself for every possible reaction he might have, she wordlessly held her left hand out to Rick.

He caught her hand in his and stared open-mouthed at the diamond winking back at him. Clearly stunned, he was left speechless.

"Oh, my God!" Bonnie strolled up just then, plunked the iced tea pitcher down on the table and stared from their joined hands to the diamond ring and finally to Tracy. "You just got engaged, didn't you? Can I see?"

Swallowing and neatly avoiding Rick's eyes, Tracy swung her suddenly very heavy-feeling hand over toward the waitress. Bonnie clutched her fingers tightly and ooohed over the sizable, marquis-cut stone.

"How cool is this?" the woman demanded after a minute of purely female admiration. "Engaged, right here at my station." She grinned at both of them as if she'd been in on the happy moment all along. "This has never happened to me before. It's so romantic! Wait'll the boss hears about this. Gosh, you guys, congratulations."

"Thanks, but..." Tracy said.

"Dessert's on the house," Bonnie said with delighted enthusiasm. "Your choice. Apple pie or chocolate cake?"

Tracy didn't know what to say. She didn't want to hurt Bonnie's feelings or ruin her jubilant mood, but on the other hand, she didn't want to accept chocolate cake under false pretenses, either. She shot a quick look at Rick as if looking for a clue as to how to respond.

He stared at her for a long, thoughtful minute, then turned his gaze on the still-smiling waitress. "That's nice of you, Bonnie. I think my fiancée and I would both vote for the cake."

Four

___

"**Y**ou got it, honey," she said, and grinning, spun on her heel and took off.

"Why'd you do that?"

"No reason to spoil her fun," Rick said as he shifted his gaze to her surprised features. "Although I never thought I'd use the words *my* and *fiancée* in the same sentence. Now that we're alone again...thought you said there wasn't a boyfriend in the picture?"

"There isn't," she said, keeping her head down and concentrating on her dinner.

"Uh-huh." That statement didn't make him

feel the least bit better. *Someone* had given her that damned ring. Rick scowled at his plate. He wasn't sure why, but when he'd first seen the rock she flashed at him, a sinking sensation had opened up in the bottom of his stomach. Though why the hell it should matter to him if Tracy Hall was engaged or not, he didn't have a clue.

Clearing his throat, he asked, very reasonably he thought, "Then, who gave you that ring?"

She glanced up at him, winced and immediately lowered her gaze again. Shrugging, she said, "I haven't decided yet."

Rick closed his eyes briefly and mentally counted to ten. He got as far as three before saying, "All right, I've got to know. What the hell is going on, Tracy?"

Deliberately, she set her fork down, took a sip of tea, then sat back and looked at him. Cradling the ring in her lap, she said, "Just what we were talking about a few minutes ago."

"More," he prodded, completely confused

now. When had they discussed surprise engagement rings?

"Okay. Look, Rick," she said on a long, indrawn breath. "Remember how you said we'd be adrift in a sea of happily married couples at the reunion?"

"Yeah..." And what that had to do with diamond rings from nobody, he couldn't have said.

"Well, I just decided to get into a life boat instead, that's all."

That sure cleared things up.

"I'm still lost," he told her. Watching her expression shift and change in the soft light was hypnotizing. She'd never make a good poker player, he thought absently. Everything she was feeling showed on her face. At the moment, she seemed to be torn between embarrassment and anticipation.

"It's simple," she said and took another bite of chicken. She chewed it thoroughly, driving Rick nuts waiting for her to swallow and get back to the point at hand. "I am not going to face all of those people who knew me as Queen Nerd of the Universe without a ring on my finger.''

He snorted. ''A rabid feminist, I see.''

''This has nothing to do with feminism,'' she countered, leaning across the table. ''This is just about me. *My* life. Or lack thereof.''

''Tracy...''

''No, you wanted to hear this, so listen to all of it.''

''Fine.'' Appetite gone, he pushed his plate to one side and gave her his undivided attention.

''You don't know what it was like,'' Tracy said softly and even in that strained whisper, he caught the tiny thread of old aches. '''Poor Tracy,''' she mimicked, her voice a reedy falsetto. '''Couldn't catch a man with a bear trap.''' She shook her head. ''No way am I going back there to listen to that stuff again. I can't stand having to see pitying glances tossed my way all weekend.''

A twinge of regret pierced him as he recalled the teenaged Tracy. Being young and stupid himself at the time, he'd never given a moment's thought to how she was feeling. All he'd been interested in was getting rid of her so he could spend time with the lovely Meg.

Which just went to show how shortsighted the young really are.

A vague, time-misted memory of her adolescent features rose up in his mind. Oversize glasses continually slipping down her freckled nose. Braces, baggy sweatshirts, ponytail and holey tennis shoes. He smiled slightly at the portrait. But that image slowly faded away and was replaced by the face of the woman sitting across from him.

Her smooth complexion flushed with twin red patches on her cheeks, her blue eyes shone brightly with indignation or excitement, he wasn't completely sure which. But her lips trembled slightly and he had a feeling that an impending smile was *not* the reason.

"Trust me, Trace," he said wryly, "nobody's going to look at you and say 'poor Tracy.'"

"A lot you know. And that's not even

counting my mom," Tracy went on as if she hadn't paused at all.

"What's your mom got to do with this?" he wondered aloud. "She's terrific."

Tracy smiled and nodded. "Granted. She is that. On the downside, I am heartily tired of having to tell that very terrific lady, 'No Mom, I haven't met a nice man yet.'"

He smothered a grin he knew she wouldn't appreciate. But he knew just what she was talking about. His conversations with his own mother had gotten a little strained in the last year or so. Patty Bennet wanted grandchildren before, as she so gently put it, "you have to drag them kicking and screaming to a nursing home to visit me."

And if he was to be honest, every once in a great while, he too wished he didn't lead such a solitary life.

But damn it, why should someone like Tracy have to resort to an imaginary fiancé? "So instead, you're going to lie to her?"

Her spine stiffened so abruptly, it looked as though some unseen hand had shoved a pole down the back of her blouse. "It's not exactly a lie," she said. "More like allowing her to see the ring and draw her own conclusions."

She was really something. And for some reason, it did his heart good to know that snappy clothes and trendy haircut aside, the real, irrepressible Tracy was alive and well.

"Yeah?" Fascinated now in spite of himself, Rick played devil's advocate. It was a crazy plan. Couldn't possibly work. There were too many variables. You'd think a math whiz like her would have spotted them. "And what do you say when Mom asks who the lucky man is? Going to let her decide that on her own, too?"

"No."

How did she get that prim, small-town librarian set to such full, luscious-looking lips? he wondered. "Then you are going to lie to Mom. And Dad. And Sister. And entire town."

She paled slightly and her blue eyes widened. "Good grief. You make it sound awful."

He grinned. She looked so guilty. "Just dangerous."

"How?"

"Somebody's bound to find out, Tracy. You're not exactly one of the champion liars of the western world." At least, she didn't used to be, he told himself. Could her character have changed as much as her outward appearance? Then she spoke, reassuring and worrying him all at once.

"I could be," she argued. "With a little practice."

That would be a shame, he thought. He already knew way too many women who could lie like election-bound politicians. They were so busy saying what they thought he wanted to hear, he never found out who they really were.

Tracy, he was quickly discovering, was a woman he'd like to know *a lot* more about.

"Besides," he said as if she hadn't spoken at all, "what happens when the long-awaited wedding doesn't happen?"

Instantly, she relaxed a bit and gave him a

smile that lit up his insides like a fireworks display on the Fourth of July. He sucked in a breath, hoping to cool the fires. It didn't help.

He'd have to work on that.

"That's the best part, really," she confided. "See, a month or so after the reunion, I'll call my folks and tell them that I've cancelled the wedding."

He shook his head at her. She really had been planning this for a while. "But won't that bring on a new onslaught of 'Poor Tracey's?'"

"Nope." She gave him another brilliant smile and this time the warmth that flooded him didn't catch him by surprise. It still worried him, though. "*I* will have ended it, so no sympathy will be required."

"Amazing," he muttered.

"Isn't it?"

The most amazing thing of all was that she'd had to come up with the stupid plan in the first place. Why weren't there a dozen drooling men hanging all over her? How could a woman who looked as good as Tracy remain unattached for so long? And why was he spending so much time noticing just how good she looked?

Rick had wanted to use this driving trip to do some relaxing. To clear his head. Instead, all he'd thought about since the first time he'd seen her was Tracy's legs. Tracy's smile. Tracy's eyes.

Were her eyes really that blue? Or did she have those specially tinted contact lenses? Surely nobody's eyes could be such a clear, electric blue. Or, he thought with a pang, hold such innocence.

"So why tell me the truth?" he asked quietly.

"Well," she said, looking pointedly at the ring on her finger. "I have to get used to wearing the thing, don't I?"

"I suppose." He deliberately avoided looking at it. Pretend engagement or not, for some reason, he didn't care to think about Tracy having a fiancé.

"And," she continued, "we've got a three-day trip home. I thought that maybe along the way, you could help me dream up my personal Prince Charming.''

When he simply looked at her, she blurted out, ''For old time's sake? One friend to another?''

Friends? Is that what they were?

They hadn't seen each other in years. How could they be friends? And their relationship when they were kids could hardly be classified as chummy. Then there was his physical response to her. No other woman he'd ever known had had the ability to torch his body with a look. A smile.

Were those the reactions of a *friend?*

Mercifully, he was saved from having to answer right away. Their waitress, Bonnie, accompanied by three more waitresses, approached their table.

''Oh no,'' he muttered, studying those smiling faces.

''What?'' Tracy asked, then shifted her gaze to follow his. ''Good grief,'' she whispered.

Beaming at each of them in turn, Bonnie

set two thick slices of chocolate cake down on the table and lit the tiny birthday candle she'd plunked into each piece.

"Bonnie..." Tracy said softly.

"This is a celebration, honey," the waitress assured her.

Tracy looked at Rick.

Rick looked at Tracy.

The waitresses launched into a rousing rendition of "Congratulations to You," sung to the familiar birthday tune. Soon, other customers joined in until the restaurant rang with their slightly off-key musical good wishes.

The blush on her cheeks was sweet. The shine in her eyes was endearing. And a small chip of ice fell from around his heart.

Rick's and Tracy's gazes met and locked in silent embarrassment and a partnership was born.

By the time they reached their motel, it was late and Tracy was exhausted. Stumbling up the stairs, she stopped in front of her room and blindly scraped the key across the lock until it slipped in. Turning it, she stepped into the darkened room and took a long, deep breath. The sharp odor of disinfectant tickled her nose and she wrinkled it in response.

Rick followed her in, carrying one of her bags along with his own. He sniffed experimentally and said, "At least we know they're clean."

She flopped down onto the mattress. "At this point, I wouldn't care if it was a tent with a dirt floor. As long as it came with a bed."

He chuckled and hit the nearby light switch. A puddle of lamplight brightened a small patch of the room. Setting her bag down on the floor, he said, "According to the sign in the lobby, they offer free coffee and Danish pastry in the morning. Want me to bring you some when I get mine?"

With effort, she lifted her head from the mattress and looked at him blearily. "And what time would that be?"

He smiled and Tracy willed her stomach to stop spinning in response. "I want to get an early start," he told her.

"How early is early?" she asked, flicking a quick glance at the bedside clock radio. Only ten o'clock. She felt like it was three in the morning. But then, she wasn't really big on nightlife.

"I figured to get up about six, be on the road by seven."

"Seven. You mean a.m.?"

His chuckle rippled the air. "Does that mean yes, you will require coffee?"

"A gallon or so should do it," she muttered, letting her head drop back to the bed. "Black. As much as you can carry."

"Aye-aye ma'am," he said and took a step toward the door. "G'night Tracy."

"Uh-huh." She yawned.

"Lock the door behind me before you fall asleep."

Her eyes closed. She had to remember to take out her contacts. "Oh, yes, sir, Captain, sir."

She thought she heard him laugh again, but couldn't be sure. A moment later, he was gone, headed for his own room next door.

She sighed and settled into the bed, letting its too-soft mattress reach up and drag her into sleep.

A series of brisk knocks rudely interrupted her slide into unconsciousness. "Go away."

"Lock the door, Tracy."

His voice was muffled, but still clear. And she had the feeling that Rick was just stubborn enough to stand right there all night until she got up and followed orders. Grumbling under her breath, she shoved herself to her feet, stumbled across the room and slammed her toe into the table leg. A grunt of pain erupted from her throat.

"Are you all right?"

"Dandy," she said, wincing as she loudly twisted the dead bolt into place. "Happy now?"

"Dandy," he said. Then a few quick steps told her he was gone.

It took only a minute or two to shed her clothes and set the alarm for the disgusting hour of 6:00 a.m. Then Tracy dragged herself to the bathroom and took out the contacts that felt like two slabs of tile. Finally, she wandered back to the main room, fell face first onto the bed and gave herself up to oblivion.

Soft yet vivid rose-colored clouds streaked across the morning sky as the sun moved higher and higher. Six-thirty and Rick was ready to go. He'd already checked them out of their rooms, stowed his things in the car and enjoyed a leisurely cup of coffee as he gave Tracy time to wake up.

Of course, he'd needed a little extra time himself that morning. Despite the comfortable room and the too-soft mattress, he hadn't gotten much sleep. Dreams of Tracy kept dancing through his sub-conscious.

Dangerous, he knew, but he'd been helpless to stop the parade of images racing across his mind. Tracy Hall had no business visiting his dreams. She was simply a favor he was doing for Meg. An old acquaintance. A kid.

Yeah, he told himself. A kid with legs like a runway model's.

"Oh, perfect," he grumbled aloud and continued up the stairs from the motel lobby, moving toward her room. Nothing was going to happen between him and Tracy. They'd spend a few days together. Attend the reunion. Visit with family. Then go on about their lives. Probably wouldn't see each other again for another ten years or so.

He scowled to himself at that thought, then immediately wondered why the idea of losing touch with Tracy Hall should bother him. Then again, maybe some things were better left unexplored.

Twin cellophane-wrapped Danish pastries in his pocket, Rick looked from the two large disposable cups of coffee he held to Tracy's closed door. Sighing, he gave the door a couple of gentle kicks.

No answer.

''You've had an extra half hour, Trace,'' he muttered. ''Time to get up.'' The sooner they got on the road, the sooner they'd be in Oregon and he'd be able to relax. At least until the ride home. He kicked the door again and this time was rewarded by the muffled sound of her voice.

"I'm coming! Don't get your hump over the dashboard!"

What? Where the heck had she gotten that one? One corner of his mouth lifted in a smile that froze on his face when she yanked the door open. His throat went dry and he was fairly certain his heart stopped. Outlined in the open doorway, stood Tracy, naked but for the skimpy, motel-issue towel wrapped around her incredibly curvy figure.

As if his imagination hadn't done enough damage to his sleep-deprived body, here she was in living color. His gaze swept over her quickly, noting the droplets of water clinging to her bare, tanned shoulders and the tendrils of damp hair lying along her flushed cheeks.

Oh, he needed help. Fast.

"Rick?" she asked hesitantly, then added, "I sure hope it's you."

"Hope?" he asked, noting that she was staring blindly. Irritated, he swung around to make sure no one else was enjoying his view of her. But the place was deserted this early in the morning.

"Thank God. It is you." Her squint deepened, as if that would help. "Who can see this early in the morning?" She sniffed once or twice and a beatific smile lit up her features. "Coffee. My hero."

She reached out in his direction and Rick moved the cup into range. Her fingers curled around the cup and brought it close to her face. She pulled in a deep breath, savoring the aroma of the freshly brewed coffee before taking a small sip and letting the beverage roll down her throat. It was almost as though he was watching a religious experience.

Which was certainly a better idea than watching her scantily clad body.

He cleared his throat loudly, hoping to dislodge the hard knot of need clogging it. "So you didn't know it was me, you just opened the door to whoever. Wrapped in a towel."

She shoved her hair back from her face. "I'm covered." She glanced down. "Aren't I?"

"Barely." The single word scraped past his throat.

"Geezz, Captain," she pointed out grumpily. "I wear less on the beach."

"That's different," he snapped, not even wanting to entertain the image of her shape in a bikini.

"How?"

Because a towel was so easily removed and tossed to the floor, he thought and felt his body tighten in anticipation.

"Come on in," she said and backed up a step. "It's too early to argue."

"I'll wait for you downstairs," he said, figuring it would be wise to keep his distance.

"Don't be silly," she told him. "Keep me company while I get ready." She took another slow sip of coffee, pursing her mouth on the lip of the cup. Rick swallowed heavily.

"Oooh, that's good," she murmured, turning around and heading back across the room.

There was no way to leave without admitting to Tracy that he was sorely tempted by her. Besides, he was a marine. A Devil Dog.

Trained to adapt to any life-threatening situation. The fact that this particular situation was more a threat to his self-control shouldn't matter. Should it?

"Ooh-rah," he muttered, stepped inside and closed the door behind him. He could do this. What was a few minutes, more or less? All he had to do was picture Tracy as the pony-tailed, braces-sporting nemesis of his youth. That should do it.

And that vow lasted about ten seconds—the length of time it took him to notice that the bottom of her towel just barely covered the curve of her behind as she walked away from him. He bit back a groan then winced as she bumped into the sharp corner of the TV table bolted to the wall. But she hardly paused before continuing on with a slight limp. "Didn't that hurt?" he asked.

"What? Oh. No." She set her coffee down on the bathroom counter and leaned in close to the mirror.

Rick inhaled sharply and looked away from

her curves. When she leaned, that towel crept up way too high for his peace of mind.

"I'll only be a few more minutes," she said.

He spared her a quick glance and noted the sheet of paper she was taping to the bathroom mirror. "What are you doing?"

"Getting beautiful," she mumbled. "It's quite a production, you know."

"Really?" Conversation, *any* conversation was better than letting his mind run amok.

"Yeah, look." She waved a hand at him in the mirror, urging him closer.

His fingers tightened on his coffee cup as he moved up beside her. *Steady Marine... steady.*

She reached for a pair of glasses, slipped them on and studied the paper for a long minute before picking up a small pot of what looked like peach-coloured powder. Then, a long handled brush in her hand, she swept the makeup over her cheeks until she looked as though her face had been sun-kissed.

"I bought all of this stuff a couple of weeks

ago,'' she muttered, checking the paper before reaching for yet another tub of cosmetic. ''The consultant wrote everything down for me. All I have to do is follow it. Like those paint-by-number kits we used to get as kids.''

''Uh-huh.'' He moved aside, keeping two feet of space between them. A narrow, but safe margin.

He studied her in the glass as she applied layer after layer of makeup. It didn't look bad, he thought. Despite the number of coats of war paint, she still looked natural, un-made-up. So what, he wondered, was the point?

To his way of thinking, she really didn't need any of the stuff. Even fresh from the shower, she damn near glowed with healthy beauty. Her softly tanned skin shimmered in the fluorescent lights. Behind her glasses, her blue eyes looked wide and beautiful—answering one of his questions from yesterday. That clear, shining blue wasn't enhanced by colored lenses.

It was simply Tracy.

A part of her, every bit as much as her

friendliness to waitresses and her innocent staging of a pretend engagement. All simply Tracy. All simply driving him out of his mind.

Despite his best efforts, his gaze dropped slightly to where her towel was knotted between her breasts, lush and full beneath the limp cotton covering.

Simply Tracy.

Simply big trouble.

Five

———

By midday, Tracy's behind ached, her eyes were like twin burning coals, and even the scenery had lost some of its charm. With hardly any traffic on the wide, smooth highway, they'd sailed up the coast, cruising through San Luis Obispo, Paso Robles and up through Salinas. One mile stretched into the other; towns sped by with hardly a notice. She hadn't even paid attention to Gilroy, the garlic capital of the world, beyond taking the precaution of rolling her window up until they were safely past.

And, Tracy'd pretty much given up trying to talk to Rick. For some reason, he'd hardly said a word to her since they'd left the motel that morning.

She shot him a covert look and noted with some disgust that his jaw looked tight. He must be clenching his teeth hard enough to bite through a nail. Well, what was he so mad about?

It wasn't *him* who'd been caught wearing nothing but a towel and ugly, clunky glasses. Of course, at the time, she hadn't thought much of it. She'd been in such a rush to get ready and there was the makeup pie chart to follow and coffee to drink and all.

But now that she thought about it, Tracy realized that Rick's friendly attitude shift had really coincided with him finding her practically naked.

Her eyebrows arched high on her forehead as she gave some thought to that notion. Could it be she'd made him nervous? In the next instant, her brain laughed at the idea. Right. She'd made such a seductive picture, after all. Wet hair, half her face made up and wearing those glasses that made her look like Adam Ant.

Get a grip, Trace. He wasn't struck dumb by desire. She'd probably just scared him to death. May have put him off women for the rest of his life.

It wasn't fair, she thought, for her to still feel such an enormous attraction to the man. Especially when she knew darn well it would never go anywhere. Because, except for a shared past, they really had nothing in common.

She shivered slightly as a cold wind raced past her shoulders and touched the back of her neck with icy fingers. Leaning forward a bit, she rolled her window up halfway.

Living in Southern California for so long had made her blood too thin. It seemed her body had forgotten how different things were farther north. Even now, in the middle of June it was chilly enough that Tracy was glad she'd worn her new raspberry-colored cable knit pullover sweater. Her ivory twill slacks weren't especially warm, but as long as the Range Rover's heater kept puffing at her toes, she'd be fine.

Besides, it wasn't just the weather making things so chilly around here.

Frowning, she shifted her gaze back to the stoically silent man beside her. His eyes were hidden from her behind those blasted aviator sunglasses. Not that he'd glanced at her since stopping for gas an hour ago. Nope. He'd kept his face forward, eyes on the road.

Well, they had at least two more days of travel to live through and she wasn't going to spend them with the human equivalent of the Sphinx. He didn't have to like her, but he could at least *talk*.

"What is your problem?" she asked abruptly, shattering the silence.

"Me? I don't have a problem." His tone said different. That and the fact that now a muscle was twitching spasmodically in his jaw.

"Then why so cheerful?" She turned in her seat so that she was facing him. "You know, you really ought to hold down the hijinks. It's not safe to be driving while having such a good time.''

''Very funny.''

''One of us has to be.''

''Look, Tracy, is it all right with you if I just don't feel like talking?'' At last, he spared her a quick look. But those sunglasses hid whatever he was thinking. She wondered idly if that was the precise reason he wore them. ''Not all of us,'' he added, ''feel the constant need to fill a silence.''

''Constant?'' she echoed, astonished. ''You haven't said a word to me since the gas station, when, if I remember correctly, you graciously asked, 'Pull the damn car up farther, will you?''

She thought she saw a flicker, a twitch of his lips, but it was gone so fast, she couldn't be sure.

But he nodded and acknowledged. ''Okay. So I've been a little unsociable.''

''A *little?*''

Another twitch of his lips that slowly lifted into a half smile. "All right, a lot."

Well, it wasn't much of a conversation, she thought. But it was something. "Why?"

His features settled briefly into stone again. "No reason."

"Oh, good grief," she muttered. One step forward, two back. "Are you this communicative with your troops? Have the Marines taken up mind reading?"

"When I have something to say," he told her, "I'll say it."

"Alert the media," she muttered darkly. Really. She should have just taken the train. But in the next instant, she reminded herself that she didn't like trains much better than planes. And besides, a small voice whispered inside her, miserable mood or not, Rick Bennet was better company than strangers.

"Check the map for me, Tracy," he said, ignoring her little comment. "We'll be heading into the city soon and I don't want to get in the wrong lane and end up sucked into the traffic heading onto the Oakland Bay Bridge."

Well at least she knew the Captain was still capable of giving orders. If she hadn't been in a moving car, she might have leapt to her feet and snapped him a salute.

Although, she had to give him a few points here. He obviously wasn't one of those men who thought that women couldn't read maps. That said something for him, didn't it?

Dutifully, she picked up the neatly folded pages and ran one fingertip along the route of Highway 101 until she came to the outskirts of San Francisco. The jumble of red lines and blue came together and spun outward again like the tangled threads of an unraveling tapestry.

Following them, she noted the streets they'd have to take through the heart of San Francisco to get to the Golden Gate Bridge.

"Check the turn-off for old Route 1, too," he said. "It's on the other side of the bridge."

"I know." Surprised, Tracy turned her head to look at him. "We're not staying on 101?"

"Uh, no," he said and looked over his left shoulder before changing lanes.

"Why? Highway 101's much quicker. Probably save a day of riding." Not to mention the road being a heck of a lot straighter than the hairpin curves and twists and dips of the older roads.

For years, Route 1 had been the only way to drive north on the coast. Then some wonderful engineers had come up with something better. Sure, the scenery wasn't as gorgeous as the old road. In fact, no other highway in the country could compare to the sights seen on Route 1. But only the strongest stomachs survived that old two-lane road unscathed. And Tracy's stomach didn't come close to qualifying.

His hands tightened on the wheel until his knuckles gleamed white against his tanned flesh. "I considered it, but the whole reason I drove to this reunion instead of flying was so that I could take a leisurely ride up the coast. Enjoy some R and R." He swallowed hard, shot her a look, then added, "No reason to change my plan, right?"

And yet, he'd considered changing it. He just admitted as much. Why? Was the idea of getting rid of her company a day earlier than he'd planned that enticing? Well, he certainly knew how to make a girl feel special.

But she was jumping to conclusions, wasn't she? Who said she'd had anything at all to do with his plans? After all, she was little more than a hitchhiker. Like the luggage in the trunk, she went where he went.

But she wasn't looking forward to that hellishly twisted road.

San Francisco was as crowded as he remembered it. Parts of it were charming, but mostly it was just another big city, with its good and bad areas.

Thousands of cars clogged the narrow streets and every time a light changed, they lurched forward and stopped again in a huddled mass, like some demented herd of lemmings.

Rick grumbled under his breath, wished he hadn't quit smoking a year ago and threw a quick glance at Tracy. She didn't seem to mind the traffic. Instead, she had her window down and half her upper body leaning out. Clearly, she was enjoying both the cold ocean wind and the busy hustle around them.

He smiled thoughtfully as he watched her and he felt his tension sliding way. Hard to be frustrated with bumper-to-bumper traffic when watching her watch the city. She might be hard on his self-control, but she was sure easy on the eyes.

Another car pulled up next to them on Tracy's side and stopped for the light.

"Hi there, gorgeous," a deep voice called out over the blast of rock and roll pouring from his radio.

Rick scowled, stiffened and inched the car forward.

"Hello," Tracy answered.

Did she have to sound so damned friendly?

"In town for long?" the guy asked.

"Just passing through," she said.

What the hell was the guy thinking? Couldn't he see Rick sitting right there? For all that man knew, Tracy was his wife and yet there the idiot sat, flirting for all he was worth.

Easing up on the brake, Rick moved the car forward another inch or so, hoping to take Tracy far enough from her admirer to end their conversation.

No such luck.

"How about meeting me for a cup of coffee before you pass through?"

Rick shot the man a glare, but the guy only had eyes for Tracy.

"Oh," Tracy told him with a shake of her head, "I don't think I can. But thanks."

Rick leaned forward in his seat until he had a better look at Romeo, sitting in his low-slung BMW convertible. Giving the man a stare that should have immolated him on the spot, Rick snarled, "Yeah. *Thanks.*"

And still the guy had the nerve to ignore him and wink at Tracy. "Enjoy your trip, pretty lady," he called out as Rick deliberately forced his way into another lane.

"He was *flirting* with me," Tracy said as she sat back in her seat.

"You noticed." Why did she sound so damned surprised? Hadn't she looked in the mirror lately?

"It was so nice of him."

"Oh, yeah. Real thoughtful." He whipped off his sunglasses and glared at her. "Lord, Tracy. The guy could be an ax murderer."

She laughed at him. "Paranoid much?" Then she shook her head and those damned blond curls of hers danced around her face. "Relax, Rick. He was just flirting." She grinned and added, "With *me*."

"Yeah. With *me* sitting right here." Still grumbling, he turned face front again. "The guy's a jerk."

Tired of the conversation, and worried about his own reaction to the traffic-snarled Lothario, Rick concentrated on the car in front of him and followed along like a good little lemming.

Damn it, why did *he* care if strangers flirted

with Tracy? Why did it bother him that she flirted right back?

And why was he thinking about it?

Beside him, Tracy leaned forward as they neared the Golden Gate. He sensed her excitement and some of his frustration eased. Sparing her a quick look, he briefly enjoyed the anticipation written on her features.

And then they were atop the bridge and the Pacific Ocean stretched out far below them and into the distance. The overhead cables seemed to sway in the high wind and the pedestrians hiking along the edges of the bridge bent into the stiff breeze, heads bowed as if in prayer.

Off to the right, the city glittered white under the sun.

"Isn't this great?" she whispered, straining to see past him to the open ocean.

He followed her gaze with a quick glance, noting the boats dotting the surface of the water, their colorful sails looking like jewels dropped from above.

"When we were kids," Tracy said, still

turning one way then the other, so she wouldn't miss anything, "Dad used to tell Meg and me that Godzilla lived here, in the bay."

He laughed outright. "Godzilla?"

"Oh, yeah." She flashed him a brilliant smile that nearly left him breathless. "And more importantly, Godzilla loved the color red and was always watching for red cars."

Sounded like something her dad would do.

Still chuckling, Rick shook his head and said, "As I remember, your folks drove a red station wagon."

"Yep." They were at the top of the suspension bridge now and Tracy leaned out her window, trying for a better look. Then she pulled back inside and finished her story. "So Dad put Meg and me in charge of watching for Godzilla. You couldn't have pried our faces from the windows when we crossed this bridge."

"Scared, huh?"

"Only a little. Mostly, we just wanted to see Godzilla up close and personal." Pushing her hair back from her wind-kissed face, she sighed and said, "It was always fun. Going places with them."

Family vacations. The kind of thing he would never experience again. A pang of regret surprised him. To cover it, he said, "Now Meg's probably telling her kids the same stories."

"Yeah," Tracy whispered and he heard a matching tone of regret echoing in her voice.

For some reason, she faded into silence after that and Rick left her to her thoughts. Lord knew, he had plenty of his own to occupy him. Like what he was going to do about the Tracy-inspired fantasies that kept playing through his mind.

He had to find a way to stop them. Tracy Hall wasn't a "fling" kind of woman. And he wasn't a forever kind of man.

Was he?

"Rick!" she said sharply a few hours later. "Stop the car!"

Stop the car? He glanced at her and saw

that her face looked milky pale and carried just the slightest tinge of green.

The two-lane highway didn't afford many pull-outs, but he found one as soon as possible, whipped the Range Rover into it and slammed it into park.

Instantly, Tracy unhooked her seatbelt, opened the door and stumbled off a few feet.

He was after her like a shot. By the time he caught up with her, she was leaning against a slab of granite that looked as though it had been there since the beginning of time.

"Are you all right?" He reached for her, but she shook her head, swallowed heavily and held out one hand palm up toward him.

"I will be," she said with more confidence than her expression warranted.

Realization dawned in a flood of memories. "You still get car sick?"

She grinned weakly. "Apparently."

"Why didn't you say so?"

"What good would it have done?"

"Why'd you want to drive home, then?"

he asked, watching her expression for signs that she was feeling better.

She swallowed heavily. ''When you get plane sick, train sick and car sick, what choice do you have?''

''For Pete's sake, Tracy! If you'd reminded me, I would have stayed on 101.''

''Could we fight later?'' she asked. ''I'm not at my best right now.''

Instantly, he felt like a total ass. Nothing like yelling at somebody who's about to toss her cookies.

Well, this was going to be a fun ride. Him tied up in sexual knots and Tracy hanging her head out the window. He told himself they'd stop at the first store they spotted. Invest in some Dramamine. And by the look in her eyes, he figured three or four boxes of the stuff should be enough.

''Take some deep breaths,'' he advised in the meantime. ''In through the nose, out through the mouth.''

''Yes, sir, Captain,'' she muttered and bent

forward, hands on her knees. In between breaths, she moaned piteously.

Ruefully, he admitted, "Guess that did sound like an order, didn't it?"

She didn't look up. "You're obviously used to giving them."

"Part of the job," he agreed, and laid one hand on her back. "But I try not to do it to civilians."

"And we appreciate it," she said softly before slowly, carefully, straightening up.

"Better?" he asked, studying her face and noting that she looked a bit less green than before.

"A relative term I'm afraid," she said and swallowed heavily. "But, yeah. I think so." She lifted her head into the ferocious ocean wind and pulled in a deep breath.

Rick's gaze locked on her face, eyes closed, full lips parted as if awaiting a kiss. The wind tossed her short curly hair with abandon and he fisted his hands in his pockets to keep from reaching out to spear his fingers through the soft, wild mass.

Several cars roared past them on the highway, taking the mountainous curves at a speed that was, if not dangerous, at least terrifying. But Tracy didn't pay them the slightest attention. Several more moments passed before she opened her eyes and looked at him. Giving him a wan smile, she nodded. "Okay, I'm as ready to go as I'll ever be."

"We'll stop for Dramamine as soon as we can," he said.

"Good plan," she said. "I took my last two yesterday."

"Or," he offered sympathetically, "we can turn around and go back to 101."

She shifted her gaze out to the raw, wild seascape spread out in front of them. Waves crashed and pounded on jagged rocks. Sea spray flew into the air, catching the sun's light and shining like fistfuls of diamonds. Seabirds wheeled and screamed overhead. Clouds scuttled across a sky so blue it hurt to look at it.

After a long moment, she turned her gaze back to his. "No. It's been so long since I was up here, I'd like to take the ocean route."

"Are you sure?" he asked, despite being pleased at her decision.

"Uh-huh. But let's get that Dramamine, okay?"

"You got it." He took her hand and drew her back to the car. Opening the door for her, he eased her inside, then closed it. Leaning both hands on the open window frame, he said, "Until then let's keep your mind too occupied to pay attention to your stomach."

"And how do we do that?"

"Well, we still haven't come up with your dream man, have we?"

Her face brightened and it went against the grain to know that her smile was meant for an imaginary fiancé.

"You're right."

"Ask my troops," he told her as he walked around the front of the car. "They'll tell you I usually am."

Tracy kept her gaze fixed straight ahead. She tried not to think about the twisting road or the sheer drop-off to the ocean on their left.

"Okay," she said as Rick steered the car with all the aplomb of a race-car driver at Indy, "I guess we'll start with his name. I've decided to call him Brad."

"*Brad?*"

She risked a glance at her companion in time to see his mouth twist in distaste. "It's a perfectly good name, and with all of the Brad Pitt associations, it has a sort of panache, I think."

"It's a dork name," he said flatly.

"It is not. Brad Pitt probably never had a dorky day in his life." And speaking as a dork, Tracy knew what she was talking about.

"Fine. He's your fiancé. If you don't care, why should I?"

"Exactly." Her fingers gripped the armrest as he negotiated a turn. Her stomach did a slow slide and she started talking again, keeping her mind off it. "Okay!" she said a little forcefully and immediately quieted her voice. "So the next problem is, what does my mystery man do for a living?"

"Self-made millionaire?" Rick asked, a bit snidely, she thought.

"Actually," Tracy said, "no. Though I hesitate to admit this to a man in the military, most women love a man in uniform. And, since I want my former classmates to be pea green with envy for a change, I've decided to make Brad a Marine."

A smug smile drifted briefly across his face.

"And I'm making him a fighter pilot to boot."

The smile disappeared in the blink of an eye.

"Fighter jocks are wimps, Tracy."

"Didn't you ever see *Top Gun*?"

He snorted.

"The Blue Angels..." she said dreamily, mentioning one particular team of stunt-flying fighter pilots. She'd attended one of their shows once years ago and had been struck as dumb as everyone else in the audience that day by their courage and faultless flying skills.

"Show-offs." He dismissed their talents

with a shrug of incredibly broad shoulders. "Navy circus performers."

Well, what was he so hostile about?

"Do I detect a whiff of jealousy?"

"Not likely," he snapped and whizzed around the next turn.

"Ooohh…" she moaned gently and set the palm of her hand against her stomach.

"Sorry," he said and slowed down.

"Don't be sorry," she told him, swallowing back a wave of nausea. "Just talk to me. I thought you said you'd help me with this."

"Okay." His hands squeezed the steering wheel convulsively, his knuckles whitening repeatedly. "I'll help. But geezz. A fighter jock?"

"Why not?" she demanded, battling the queasiness in her stomach. "Women want them and men want to be them. It's perfect for my purposes. Remember," she said through gritted teeth, "I want people at home to look at me and see a whole new Tracy. And a fighter pilot will be just the thing to wave under their noses."

"Oh, for Pete's sake," he grumbled, clearly disgusted. "Don't fall for that Pilot-is-God fantasy, Trace. Any plain old, ordinary Marine is loads better than some up-in-the-air, arrogant jerk."

"Of course, you wouldn't be in the least bit biased," she pointed out from behind a tight smile.

"Of course not. Just being factual." He shot her a look from behind slightly lowered sunglasses. "It's easy to look tough thirty thousand feet up. It takes a real man to walk up to within spitting distance of the enemy and still stand his ground."

His green eyes sparkled with a fire-like brilliance that in response, set small, unbelievably hot backfires along the length of her spinal column. Staring at him now, the stern set of his jaw, the rippling muscles of his upper arms and the determined, take-no-prisoners set to his chin, Tracy was willing to concede defeat on at least this point.

There wasn't a fighter pilot in the world

who could compare with Captain Rick Bennet.

"Why do you care so much what people you haven't seen in years think of you?" he demanded, shooting her a look from the corner of his eye.

"You wouldn't understand," she said. No one who hadn't been a nerd, an outcast for most of their lives *would* understand. Certainly not a man like Rick. Mr. Popularity.

"Try me," he snapped.

"Fine," she said. "I've lived my whole life never feeling good enough," she told him and heard her voice rising as she spoke, but couldn't seem to stop it. "In grammar school, high school, college. Nowhere, no how, did I fit in. I've been ignored, pitied and endured, alternately."

"Christ, Tracy, let it go. It was years ago." He slanted another look at her, but those glasses of his hid his eyes. "You're all grown up. Successful. Beautiful. What does the past matter?"

"The past matters because that's what

shapes our futures. I can't change what's already been," she acknowledged, though there was nothing she'd like better than to go back in time and give her poor, dorky self a pep talk, "but I can change people's perceptions of me now."

"And you need a *man*—even a pretend one—to do that?"

"Yes, blast it!"

She heard the criticism in his voice, and maybe even a part of her agreed with him. But damn it, just for once, she wanted to be the girl everyone was talking about. She wanted to be the center of attention and the object of envy. Just once, Tracy wanted to be on the inside. And "Brad" was going to help her get all of that. She just knew it.

Six

___

The rest of the day's drive passed in a tense, not entirely friendly silence. She sensed Rick's disapproval coming from him in near Tsunami-proportioned waves. But she didn't need his approval for her scheme, she reminded herself and tried to ignore him. Besides, Tracy had other things to worry about, like concentrating her energies and a lot of positive thinking on keeping her stomach from rebelling.

Even the spectacular scenery did nothing to lift her misery.

They paused in a tiny town long enough to get gas and find Dramamine. When Rick suggested they have lunch and that maybe some light food would settle her stomach, Tracy only groaned.

By the time they stopped for the night, all she could think about was getting into bed and lying completely still.

The old motel, obviously built in the fifties, was a one-story job that spread out in a giant U. In the central courtyard, an ancient, weathered oak stood sentry, its gnarled limbs spreading lacy twilight shade across the parking lot.

But Tracy was in no mood to admire the place. Once inside her room, she dropped her bags and took out her contacts. She unpacked a couple of the books she'd brought with her and flopped down into the mattress. Before she could dig her glasses out of her purse, though, she was asleep. Something tapping determinedly at her consciousness woke her two hours later to a pitch-dark room.

She sighed, rolled over, and closed her eyes again.

Then the tapping started up once more and she pried one eye open.

"Whoever you are, go away," she muttered.

"Tracy?"

Rick. Knocking at the door.

Mumbling to herself, she slid off the bed and stumbled to the front door. Throwing back the bolt, she opened it to...nobody. Poking her head outside, she looked one way then the other, but the courtyard was empty. Tiny porch lights shimmered beside each of the room doors, looking like a militarily precise line of fireflies.

The knocking sounded again and this time his voice was a bit louder. "Tracy? Are you alive?"

Stepping back inside, she closed the door and glanced at the other door in the room. When she opened it, lamplight blazed into her eyes and silhouetted the man standing in the doorway.

Squinting slightly, she said, "I thought you were outside."

He stepped into her room, forcing her to back up. Only then did she notice the tray he carried. A familiar smell drifted to her and she inhaled deeply, realizing with a start of surprise just how hungry she was.

"I got adjoining rooms," he told her as he walked toward the table sitting beneath the window. Flicking on the lamp bolted to its scarred surface, he turned to look at her as she walked to join him. "You were feeling so lousy before, I..."

He stopped speaking, his voice trailing away into silence, but Tracy knew what he meant. He'd arranged for adjoining rooms in case she was still sick or needed him during the night.

It was thoughtful. And sweet. And apparently embarrassing the heck out of him, to judge by his expression. A small curl of pleasure settled low inside her. It was the first time in her life a man who wasn't her father had gone out of his way to care for her. Look after her. Surprising really, how such a small kindness could touch her so deeply.

"I brought you some chicken soup," he added.

"Smells good." She sniffed and swallowed back a rising tide of sentimentality.

"Thought you should eat something," he said. "There's ginger ale, too. Supposed to be good for upset stomachs. At least, that's what my mom always swore by."

Hers, too. Which was why now, years later, she couldn't drink the stuff without thinking of the flu. But she wouldn't tell him that.

She looked directly at the big blur across from her. "Thanks, Rick."

"No problem." He sat down in one of the chairs and waited until she was seated opposite him before saying, "Look, I'm sorry I was so hard on you earlier."

"It's okay," she said with a shrug. Picking up her spoon, she took some of the ice from her drink and dropped it into her soup bowl.

"No, it's not," he said. "It's none of my business why you want to go through with this..." he stopped and stared at her as she dropped more ice into her soup. "What are you doing?"

"Cooling it off a little."

"Oh." A heartbeat later, he started talking again. "Anyway, if you want a fighter pilot, that's fine with me."

"I didn't say I wanted one," she reminded him. "I said the women at the reunion would be impressed by one." She took a sip of soup, paused to see if her stomach would approve, then took another. Squinting up at him, she said, "But I'm willing to give a little on that point. How about just an average, everyday Marine instead?"

He grinned at her. "Ooh-rah."

"Yippee."

She reached for her drink and almost knocked it over. He caught it, displaying lightning quick reflexes, and righted it again.

"Why aren't you wearing your contacts?"

"I was asleep."

"Then where are your glasses?"

"In my purse."

''Want me to get 'em?''

''No. Thanks.'' She knew how she looked in glasses.

''Why? Wouldn't you rather see what you're eating?''

''I may be almost blind, but I can still find my mouth without looking.''

He sighed heavily. Tracy thought he shook his head, too, but it was hard to be sure. A moving blur wasn't much easier to spot than a stationary one.

She finished the soup and sat back, feeling more her old self than she had all day.

''Better?''

''Much. I may live.''

''I'm happy to hear it.''

Silence stretched on between them and Tracy was almost grateful that she couldn't see his face. What did he see when he looked at her, she wondered. Meg's sister? A half-blind klutz with a testy stomach? A successful business woman? A nerd?

A desirable woman?

Just the thought of that sent a flash of heat

sweeping through her. It felt as though every nerve she possessed was suddenly standing straight up on her skin. The cool night air did nothing to ease the warmth bubbling inside her.

"Tracy?" His voice rumbled along her spine.

"Yes?" In her imagination, he looked at her through green eyes glittering with a carefully banked passion. Her lips parted. Her throat tightened.

A long pause filled the room.

"Nothing," he said and stood up.

The scape of the chair legs against the threadbare rug signalled the end of this particular fantasy.

Narrowing her gaze further, she watched him move slowly across the room to the door that led into his room. Her heartbeat accelerated until she thought it would explode from her chest and smack him in the center of his back.

"Get some sleep," he said as he stopped in

the doorway. "If you need—well, just call me. I'll be here."

Then he closed the door.

If she needed—*what?*

Sinking back farther into her chair, she wondered what he would say if she called him back right now. If she told him exactly what she needed from him. To be held. Kissed. Made love to.

"Oh, God," she whispered and leaned forward, bracing her elbows on the table. When the glass of ginger ale tipped over, spilling icy cold liquid into her lap, she took it as a sign. Even the Fates were telling her to cool off.

"So how old is Brad?"

"Thirty, I think," Tracy said and glanced at him. "A nice, round number. Easy to remember."

"I know I'll remember Brad," Rick muttered under his breath. They'd been talking about nothing but the imaginary man for hours now. It probably wasn't possible to hate a man who didn't exist, but Rick was coming close.

Together, they'd plotted Tracy's fictitious romance with the little bastard. And though it made absolutely no sense at all, Rick knew he was jealous. Every time she said the guy's name, a new flash of irritation sputtered into life inside him.

Slanting a look at Tracy now, the grim set of his mouth softened a little. Wearing the glasses she loathed, she looked impossibly cute. Way too good for Brad.

And too damned innocent for him.

She caught his eye and asked, "What is it?"

Oh, a million things. Things he shouldn't be thinking. Feeling. Hell, he'd known her most of his life. His parents considered her one of their own. She wasn't the type of woman he could smooth into a brief, however hot, affair.

She was the marrying kind.

"Nothing," he said softly. The look in her eyes told him she didn't believe him, but wouldn't say so. Then, he heard himself add, "You look cute in glasses."

Clearly uncomfortable, she half turned in her seat, laughed shortly and shook her head. "No I don't, but those contacts hurt. So until we get home, I'll stick to these."

Exasperated, he turned his gaze back to the road. Damn it. Wasn't she aware of her allure? Didn't she have the slightest clue what she did to him? "Tracy, never argue with a man when he's telling you you're pretty."

"Cute," she corrected.

Semantics, he thought. *"Cute, pretty,* same thing."

"No, it's not," she said, settling back in her seat and folding her arms across her chest. *"Puppies* are cute. It's that whole helpless, poor-little-thing attitude all over again."

"And you got that from *cute?"* he asked. Geezz. If this was how she took a compliment, he'd have to remember not to insult her any time soon. "What are you talking about?"

"Oh, it's not your fault," she said, but her tone gave him little comfort. "Everybody does it. Always have. It's like I need protecting. Rescuing."

He was no White Knight. If anything, someone should hurry on the scene to rescue her from him. He laughed shortly both at her ridiculous statement and at the feelings rushing through him at the moment. He didn't want to rescue her. He wanted to kiss her. Hold her. Feel the soft smoothness of her skin under his palm.

Oh, for heaven's sake, he demanded silently. Why don't you just admit it? What he really wanted to do was make love to her, so completely, so thoroughly, that they were both left breathless and trembling.

Man.

He took one hand off the wheel long enough to viciously rub his jaw. Need pulsed through him. Hot. Demanding. Breathing labored, he fought against the tightening of his body and willed himself into control again. But that was getting harder and harder to do.

Not that he'd ever forced himself on a woman or anything. No. The only real danger here was that any minute now he might explode.

"I don't see what's so funny," she snapped.

"Believe me, Trace," he said wryly, "at the moment, neither do I."

A few more miles passed in strained silence until, as they rounded yet another turn in the twisted road, Tracy saw something that took her mind off Rick. She pointed off to the left and said, "Look."

A compact station wagon, its left rear tire flat as a flounder, sat dejectedly on a wide turn on the ocean side of the road. Two kids in the back seat wrestled as their mother stood beside the car alternately kicking the tire and staring off down the road as if waiting for help that wasn't coming.

Before Tracy had the chance to ask Rick to stop and offer assistance, he'd slapped on his turn blinker and slowed enough to make a dangerous U-turn onto the turnout.

"Hold on," he said as he waited for a car to pass before beginning his turn. Once it was clear, he pulled the Range Rover up behind the disabled car and turned the engine off.

"Wait here," he said, unhooking his seat-belt and opening the door.

"Oh," Tracy told him, "I don't think so." She'd seen the stranded woman's expression when they pulled up. In today's world, the poor woman didn't know whether to be relieved or terrified at their arrival.

"Huh?" he asked, glancing at her.

"I think she'll feel better if I'm along with you."

"Why would…" he stopped short and nodded. "Yeah. You're probably right. Okay, let's go."

Together, they approached the woman who had inched back toward the driver's-side door.

"Hi," Tracy called out. "Need some help?"

The woman's gaze slipped from Tracy to Rick and back again. "I guess so," she said, glancing at her kids, who were now pressing their faces to the rolled-up windows and twisting their features into weird masks. "I just called my husband..." she held up her cell phone as if to prove her statement.

Rick spoke up. "If you've got a jack and a spare, I can change the tire and maybe save your husband a trip."

Indecision clouded her features. Clearly, she wanted to accept the help, but a woman alone with two kids couldn't be too careful.

"It's okay," Tracy said, nodding her head in Rick's direction. "He's a Marine. There's nothing he likes better than to ride in like the cavalry in an old western."

The woman smiled slightly and seemed to relax a little.

Playing along, Rick gave Tracy an outraged stare. "We're way better than the cavalry. We don't even need horses."

"Oh, I know," Tracy said on a laugh. "From the Halls of Montezuma..."

"To the shores of Route 1," Rick answered.

The woman laughed softly. "Okay, I'm convinced," she said and handed Rick the keys to the car. "Everything's in the trunk."

He took the keys and she added, "And... thanks."

"No problem."

Tracy and the woman, who introduced herself as Annie Taylor, herded the two kids out of the car and back from the road as Rick went to work.

"Really," Annie said, as they perched on rocks at the turnout's edge, "I don't know what I would have done if you hadn't stopped. I did call my husband, but he wasn't home."

Tracy watched the boy and girl toss pebbles over the edge of the rock wall and smiled. "Isn't that just like a man? Never there when you need 'em."

Annie laughed. "At least *your* husband was there when I needed him."

"Oh..." Tracy started to correct her.

"A Marine, huh?" Annie mused, watching Rick hunched over the jack. "I bet he looks great in his uniform."

I bet he does, too, Tracy thought, letting her gaze slide to the man in question. Watching the muscles in his back bunch and relax beneath his blue T-shirt, she felt a tightening and release inside her. His movements were quick, sure. His big hands wielded the jack and wrench expertly and she couldn't help wondering what it would be like to have those same hands touching her body.

She shivered despite the warmth of the sun on her back. Ocean air whipped past them and Tracy dragged it deep into her lungs, forcing it past the invisible fist squeezing her chest.

"Jimmy," Annie called as her young son walked close to Rick. "Stay away from the road."

"I'm just watchin' the man," the four-year-old whined.

"He's all right," Rick assured the women.

Tracy was grateful for the distraction. Now instead of focusing on Rick, she kept a watchful eye on the two children who stared at him, fascinated.

"Why ya' doin' that, Mister?" the boy asked.

"To take the old tire off," he answered.

"But why?" the girl demanded.

"It's flat," he muttered just loud enough for Tracy to hear him.

"Why's it flat?"

"I don't know."

"You gonna blow it up?"

"No."

"Can I?"

Rick's laugh rippled through the air. "No, but you can help me with the nuts."

"Oh, boy," Jimmie crowed.

"You got nuts?" The little girl, who couldn't be more than two or three, asked. "I'm hungry."

"Not those kinds of nuts," Rick explained.

Tracy and Annie exchanged an amused, purely female glance. Women the world over found it highly entertaining to watch a man being battered by the endless stream of questions which every child knew how to deliver.

As if he knew he was being watched, he glanced at them, then let his gaze lock briefly with Tracy's. She felt the heat of that stare right down to her toes. A moment later, he and the kids were concentrating on the tire again.

When he was finished, he put the jack and the old tire into the trunk, slammed it shut, then herded the kids back to their mother before handing the keys to Annie. He brushed his dirty, grease-stained hands on the legs of his jeans and said, "The spare's a little low on air, but it should get you home with no problems."

"Thanks," she said as she steered her kids into the car again. "I mean it." Smiling at Tracy, she asked, "Do you mind?"

Understanding, she said playfully, "Just this once."

Annie nodded, walked up to Rick and gave him a quick kiss on the cheek. Then she gave him an even quicker hug and stepped back, grinning. "You were right, y'know."

Still surprised at her thank-you kiss, he asked, "About what?"

"You Marines *are* better than the cavalry."

He grinned and walked to the driver's-side door. Opening it for her, he saw her inside then closed it again. Pushing down the lock, he said jokingly, ''Remember that the next time you watch a western.''

Annie waved at both of them and drove off, her kids' voices lingering in the otherwise still air.

''''Bye, Mister...''

''I'm hungry...''

Still smiling, Tracy looked up at him.

''What?'' he asked, ''Grease on my nose?''

She shook her head. How could she explain what she was feeling? If she tried, she would have to tell him how Annie had assumed they were married and how she Tracy, had encouraged that assumption. Nope. Better to just make a joke and let it go.

''My hero,'' she said quietly and rose up on her toes to give him a brief kiss.

But the moment their lips met, something happened.

She told herself later that she must have imagined the nearly electric charge that had sizzled in the air around them and jolted along her spine, leaving her knees weak.

But at the moment, all she could do was stare at him in astonishment. Rick's green eyes darkened, going as shadowed and mysterious as a forest at midnight. And then he moved with such swiftness, Tracy's breath left her lungs in a rush.

He pulled her to him and covered her mouth with his. His lips teased and touched and explored and caressed. His hands held her firmly to him and his arms felt like bands of steel, tightening inch by inch as if he was trying to pull her body into his.

And with that kiss, in broad daylight, on the side of the road, with the sound of the ocean crashing and pounding down around them, Tracy learned exactly what she had been missing in life.

When he released her, she staggered and might have fallen if he hadn't grabbed her and guided her back to the car. He didn't speak. She couldn't speak. And once they were moving again, speeding along the highway, the silence between them only heightened the very tension that neither of them wanted to talk about.

A simple, wood-framed, one-story motel sat perched on the very edge of the ocean's door. Painted in shades of gray and a soft, neutral brown, it seemed to blend into the scenery around it. A long wooden deck marched along the front of the rooms and their footsteps echoed weirdly around them.

Tracy opened her door first, and, as she did, she gasped aloud.

Instantly, Rick was there. "What is it?"

"Look," she said simply.

The drapes on the sliding glass doors directly opposite her were pulled back, allowing the dramatic view to be the first thing a visitor saw. Beyond another wooden deck, complete with white lawn furniture and a narrow strip of neatly tended lawn, lay the Pacific Ocean.

"Wow," Rick murmured as he followed Tracy into her room.

Gray clouds lay menacingly on the far horizon, and off to the right a tower of rock rose up like the spire of some ancient, sunken castle. Spray swept up into the air as waves pounded the rock in a dance that had been ongoing for centuries.

Tracy opened the sliding glass door and stepped out onto the deck. Wind rushed at her and the sound of the ocean roared at her like a caged beast shouting defiance.

"Amazing place," Rick muttered and glanced around at the neatly swept deck and well-kept grounds. Huge chunks of rock lined the edge of the lawn as if God himself had plunked them down to create a boundary between man's world and Neptune's.

The tide was out. Tracy shifted her gaze to look at the miles-long stretch of beach winding around the point and off into the distance. Piles of driftwood tossed ashore during a storm lay stacked together like some giant child's abandoned game of Pick-Up-Sticks. Slices of silvery water traced lacey patterns on the sand, and overhead, seagulls danced in the wind.

The tensions of the last hour or so evaporated in the incredible beauty of the place, and Tracy took a long, deep breath before saying, "I'm going for a walk on the beach."

"Give me a minute," Rick said, "and I'll go with you."

She turned to look up at him. Her hair blew across her eyes and the ocean damp misted her glasses. He looked down at her with the same intensity he'd shown just before giving her the kiss of a lifetime. The memory of that kiss took her breath away. Her lips still tingled. Her hormones still raged.

It was probably a mistake to say yes. If she was as smart as everyone had always said she was, she would keep a safe distance between her and Rick. Especially now, after churning up so many emotions. But for the first time in her nerdy, brainy life, Tracy didn't want to be smart. She didn't want to think.

She wanted to feel.

Decision made, she stared up at him and said, "I'll wait."

Seven

Kids raced past them, laughing and screaming as they played hide and seek with the rippling waves lazing onto shore. An older couple walked along the water's edge, hand in hand, in companionable silence, and a teenaged boy laboriously wrote his lady love's name in the glistening sand.

They were oblivious to all of them.

The wind tugged at Tracy's lemon-yellow sweater and whipped her hair into a tangled halo around her face. She shivered and Rick pulled off his sweatshirt and laid it across her shoulders.

"Thanks," she said over the ocean's blustering thunder.

He nodded and glanced back over his shoulder at the motel. They'd walked at least a mile, and those were the first words she'd spoken to him. If he'd hoped to find a way to breach the barrier that kiss had created between them, it wasn't working.

He swallowed a groan as he remembered the moment when he'd changed things between them. When she'd kissed him, he'd simply stopped thinking. A brief, friendly kiss was all she'd meant. He'd known that in a small, rational corner of his mind. Yet with that one touch of her lips, he'd needed more. He'd needed to taste her, explore her mouth, fill himself with her. And for one moment, he'd given in to the urge that had been riding him for days now.

The fact that he'd broken the kiss quickly didn't change a damn thing.

The wind picked up, the clouds on the horizon scuttled closer, obliterating the lowering sun. One by one, the other surf walkers abandoned the strip of sand and soon they were alone on the beach. In the ocean-misted twilight, they watched as a lighthouse on a far-distant spit of land blinked reassuringly to the ships at sea.

"It's so beautiful," Tracy said softly.

Rick dipped his head to hear her over the deafening rumble around them.

"I've been away too long, I guess," she added thoughtfully.

"Yeah," he said, his gaze drifting to look past her at the broad expanse of metal-gray water. "Me too."

"Strange, isn't it?" she asked. "It's the same ocean—but in Southern California, it's so...tame. Here, it looks wild, unleashed." She shook her head as if disappointed in the words available to her for description. "So changed," she added, still trying to express what she was thinking, feeling. "So much more powerful."

He moved closer to her side, his gaze, like hers, locked on the horizon where whitecaps dotted the water's surface. She was right, he thought. In Northern California, the trees were bigger, the wind colder and the ocean more of a living, breathing presence.

But that wasn't all that had changed, he realized with a start. This afternoon, he'd watched her with those kids. Heard her laughter. Seen how the children responded to her, and it had warmed him. He'd even enjoyed the few minutes when the kids had peppered him with questions.

"Why is that, do you suppose?" she asked.

"Oh, I don't know," he said at last. "Maybe..." he turned his head to look at her. His heartbeat thundered in his ears. "Maybe, it's seeing the familiar in a different light." His gaze moved over her profile. "Maybe it's realizing that there are more sides to everything than the one we're used to seeing."

She swiveled her head and raised her gaze to his. Rick's breath left him as he stared into her blue eyes. This trip, this time together had shown him a different Tracy than the one he'd remembered. The one he'd expected. Lifting one hand, he reached out to smooth her hair back from her face. His fingertips traced along her skin, and as a jolt of heat shot down the length of his arm, he watched her eyes darken. She felt it, too.

This hum of energy when they touched.

Where did it come from? This sudden urge…need, to be with her? How was it possible that a few days in her company had him wondering about his life and the choices he'd made?

"Tracy…"

She shook her head and placed one finger across his lips in a wordless plea for silence. Then she moved into his arms and he enfolded her, drawing her close. Heart pounding, body throbbing, he stopped thinking, giving himself up to the feel of her in his arms. She rose up and angling her head, slowly replaced her finger with her mouth.

Rick groaned from deep in his throat as his arms tightened around her, pulling her as close to him as he could. He parted her lips with his tongue and swept into the warmth that he'd been dreaming about for too long. She gasped at his gentle invasion and reached up to entwine her arms around his neck.

Their tongues met in a frantic, wild dance of desire. Her breath puffed against his cheek. Her breasts flattened against his chest. His body hard and ready, when her hips rocked against him instinctively, he tore his mouth from hers to drag air into suddenly straining lungs.

''Rick,'' she murmured and her voice was carried away in the wind that buffeted them.

''I need you, Tracy,'' he told her as he lifted his head to stare down into blue eyes as glazed with passion as he knew his own to be. He needed her more than he'd ever needed anything or anyone before.

''Yes,'' she whispered brokenly. ''Oh please...''

Thunderous noise crashed through the air. The harsh cold wind wrapped itself around them and the sea inched forward to lap at their feet.

The tide had turned.

* * *

Inside her room, Rick paused long enough to draw the drapes across the sliding glass doors. The ocean's roar was reduced now to a muffled hush of sound that reverberated like a heartbeat in the room.

He turned, grabbed her and pulled her tightly against him. "There's still time to change your mind, Tracy." He whispered into her ear and prayed she wouldn't.

"I won't change my mind," she told him, and reached up to pull his head down to hers.

Their lips met in a kiss that seared him to his soul and Rick knew there would be no going back. Whatever tomorrow held, whatever else happened on this amazing trip, they would have this night. This night that had seemed destined from the first moment he'd seen her in the doorway of her condo.

Eager to touch her, to explore the body that had tormented his dreams, his hands slipped beneath the hem of her sweater. "Smooth," he murmured, "so soft."

She sucked in a gulp of air and turned her head toward his, hoping for another kiss. He

appeased her briefly and then in a swift movement, tugged her sweater up and over her
head, displaying her tanned skin and a wispy,
white lace bra.

A flush of excitement colored her cheeks.
Her eyes sparkled and her breath came in
short, sharp pants. He looked into her eyes and
held her gaze while he deftly unhooked the
front clasp of her bra and freed her breasts.
She licked her lips and the slow glide of her
tongue across her mouth ignited new fires inside him.

"Tracy..." His heartbeat staggered when
she smiled softly before slowly shrugging out
of the lacey fabric, letting the thin straps slide
along her arms until the wispy garment fell to
the floor.

No tan lines, he thought inanely and the
mental image of Tracy sunbathing in the nude
sent the force of his desire up several notches.

"Perfect," he whispered, and lifted both
hands to cup and caress her breasts and their
rose-pink tips. Instantly, her nipples stiffened

and she moaned gently as his thumbs traced back and forth across them.

"Rick," she said softly as she swayed into him, "I think my knees are giving out."

He smiled to himself. His own knees weren't any too steady. Gently, he eased her backward onto the bed and followed her down. Lowering his head, he claimed first one of her nipples, then the other, taking his time as he lavished attention on her sensitive flesh.

Tracy moved beneath him, arching her back, silently offering him more. He took it, greedily. With his lips, his tongue, the edges of his teeth, he tortured her with sweet deliberation. His own body quickened with each of her moans, sending him closer to the edge of control.

He'd never wanted a woman as badly as he wanted Tracy.

Easing away from her, Rick stood up.

"Why did you stop?" she asked, lifting her head from the mattress long enough to stare at him through wide, glazed eyes.

Just looking at her was enough to stop his heart.

"Honey," he said, "we're just getting started."

"Oh. Good." She nodded and let her head drop back onto the bed.

Quickly, Rick undressed, tossing his clothes mindlessly in his haste to return to her. Then he bent over her and slipped off her shoes, letting them fall with a soft thud to the carpet.

"Let's get your slacks off, Trace," he said quietly. "I want to feel all of you."

"Yes," she whispered and lifted her hands to fumble at the gold chain belt at her waist.

But her fingers were clumsy and Rick was too impatient now for the feel of her beneath him. He brushed her hands aside and did it himself. Undoing the belt, he unzipped her slacks and slowly tugged them down the length of her legs.

Honey-blond skin gleamed in the lamplight as he exposed inch after lovely inch. But as her slacks came away, he noticed two or three bruises marring the perfection of her body and he frowned slightly. Fingering the largest with a gentle touch, he asked, "What happened? You're black and blue."

She shook her head against the mattress. "I'm fine. I just tend to bump into things."

He smiled to himself as he remembered her crashing into a table just the other day. Bending over her, he kissed the bruised flesh and ran his tongue across her skin.

"Oh, my," she muttered thickly.

"Oh, my is right," he agreed and slipped his fingers beneath the band of her panties, tugging them down and off before lying beside her on the bed.

The flowered quilt beneath them felt cool and slick against his skin. He thought about tearing it off and lying her on the sheets, but he didn't want to waste any more time. What he wanted—what he needed—was to be buried inside Tracy. To feel her body's warm, damp, intimate caress.

He smoothed the flat of his palm up her thigh, over her hip and around to slide across her flat, honey-brown abdomen. His fingertips brushed across the neat triangle of blond curls that hid the juncture of her thighs, and Tracy's body jumped beneath his hands.

"Rick," she muttered thickly as she moved closer to him, "I need you to..."

"I know, honey," he whispered as he shifted his fingers to explore the damp heat that awaited him. "I know. We both need..."

She jumped again when his fingertips first touched her. He lowered his head to take her mouth with his and so tasted her gasp when he dipped one finger into her depths. Tracy shuddered violently and clung to him, her fingernails digging into his shoulders.

She drew her legs up and her thighs parted, granting him access, of which he took full advantage. Again and again, he stroked her secrets, loving the feel of her damp softness.

When he shifted position slightly and reclaimed one of her nipples, Tracy moaned aloud and held him more tightly than ever.

She felt as though she was poised on the edge of a cliff and the only thing keeping her safe was her grip on Rick.

And then he suckled her and even that tenuous hold nearly dissolved. Tracy's mind reeled with the sensations pouring through her body. Electrified, from the top of her head to the tips of her toes, she twisted and writhed in his grasp. Her hands explored his muscular back, then slid around to the front where her fingertips trailed unceasingly through the soft brown curls that dusted his skin.

He touched her deeply, intimately again, and she lifted her hips in an instinctive quest for more of the same. In and out, his fingers moved, pitching her higher and higher onto a plane where the air was too thin to breathe and she was too pleasure-filled to care.

It seemed she'd been waiting all her life for this night. To know it all at last. To feel a man's body linked with hers in the most ancient way. And to have Rick be the man to introduce her to things she'd never thought to know was somehow so fitting—as if Fate had planned this all along.

Emotions and sensations spiralled out of control. Her brain shorted-circuited but she didn't mind, because she couldn't think anyway, and a brain wasn't necessary to feel what she was feeling.

His thumb brushed across an incredibly sensitive piece of flesh and Tracy gasped. Shivers of anticipation coursed through her. Her legs quivered and she felt as though even her soul was holding its breath.

"Rick, I can't stand this any more..." she whispered, though she knew if he tried to stop now, she would have to kill him. "Do something. Now."

"Yes, ma'am," he said as he lifted his head to look down at her. Then he shifted position again, kneeling between her updrawn legs.

She looked up at him as he lifted her hips off the bed. She felt his body pressing against the entrance to hers. She took a breath. Held it. Then felt it slide from her lungs as he entered her.

Tight. She felt her insides stretch and widen to welcome him as he pushed himself home.

Tipping her head back into the mattress, Tracy's fingers curled into the bedspread and hung on. He was inside her. Filling her. It was as though in that one, heartrending instant, they had become one person. Two bodies fused into one.

At last, she opened her eyes and looked at him again. Perspiration dotted his brow and along with desire, she saw confusion shining in his eyes. Then she moved, rocking her hips against his. He sucked in a gulp of air and gritted his teeth. She sighed as she felt his body touch her soul.

Whatever the spell was that had held him so still was shattered. He leaned over her, bracing himself on his hands. When she began to move, Tracy moaned at the beautiful friction created between them. Slowly at first, she moved with him, matching his thrusts with her own.

The sound of the ocean's heartbeat echoed in the room. She struggled to draw air into heaving lungs as her body tightened further and further until she felt as though she might shatter like a piece of crystal flung against a rock.

This was so much better than the books had promised it would be. Every romance novel she'd ever read suddenly raced through her whirling mind. Descriptions of fireworks and inner explosions all seemed too faint-hearted for the reality of the sensations rushing through her.

And no romantic hero could have been more adept than Rick. Her heart swelled to amazing proportions. Emotion clogged her throat and quickened her pulse. The long-ago torch she'd carried for this man seemed as bright as a match flickering in the wind compared to what she felt now.

How had this happened? How had a teen-aged crush turned into love over the course of three days? Impossible, a still-rational corner of her mind screamed. Then her thoughts dissolved beneath an onslaught of rippling sensations that demanded her attention.

She opened her eyes and stared up at him, losing herself in the green eyes that captured her gaze.

It was about to happen. She knew it. Her

insides fisted. She felt a swell of anticipation building. She locked her legs around his hips, pulling him closer, harder to her as she strained to reach for the climax already engulfing her.

Leaning to one side, Rick slid his hand between their bodies and when his fingertips touched her, Tracy's body erupted. She cried out his name and clung to him desperately as she rode wave after pulsing wave of satisfaction.

Only when her whimpers had subsided did Rick groan, stiffen against her and give himself up to the same all-encompassing pleasure that had claimed her.

"Tracy?"

She stirred and mumbled something completely incoherent.

"C'mon Trace," he said, voice a little louder this time, "wake up. We have to talk."

"Sleep first," she muttered thickly and turned into him, throwing her arm across his chest. "Talk later."

Tempting, he thought. At the moment, there was nothing he'd like better than to stretch out beside her and hold her and get some sleep for the first time in days.

Then she snuggled in closer, flinging her leg over his. His body leapt into life again. Who was he trying to kid? As long as this particular woman was lying next to him, neither one of them would get any sleep. Gritting his teeth against the flash of desire rocketing through him, he moved farther away from her. They had to talk.

"Tracy, wake up." His voice held a thread of Marine in it and surprisingly enough, she responded.

Those wide, blue, not-so-innocent-now eyes opened and looked up at him. Then she smiled lazily, reaching one hand up to cup his face. "Hi."

"Hi, yourself," he muttered and tried to ignore the touch of her hand on his face.

Frowning slightly, she let her arm fall to her side and asked, "What's wrong with you?"

"Oh," he said sarcastically, "not a thing. How are you feelin'?"

She grinned and stretched, moaning softly with the movement. His jaw tightened as he watched her.

"I feel...*wonderful*," she finally said on a satisfied sigh.

"That's great." He nodded sharply and swung his legs off the bed. If he was going to be able to think, he couldn't be lying there beside her. "She feels wonderful," he muttered just under his breath. "Perfect."

Naked, he paced the narrow confines of the room. After a couple of quick trips back and forth, he chanced a look at the bed again.

Leaning back against the pillows, Tracy lay atop the flowered quilt like some Amazon queen awaiting a sacrifice offered by her loyal peasants. Her dusky, golden-tanned legs were crossed at the ankle and she'd folded her arms across her middle. Her breasts peeked at him from over her arms. How she managed to look so calm and composed while stark naked, he didn't understand.

Knowing he was about to shatter that calm did little to make him feel better. His fault. He should have taken better care of her. Should have stopped to *think*.

But how could he possibly have guessed that she was a virgin?

"What *is* the matter?" she asked, her voice as cool as the gleam in her eyes.

"Oh, not much. Just the fact that you didn't bother to tell me you were a virgin."

Her eyes widened a little. "You could tell?"

Unbelievable. "Of course I could tell." In fact, when that little surprise presented itself, he'd been shocked enough to consider pulling away from her. Of course that consideration had lasted only until the next moment, when she'd moved against him, taking him farther inside her. But the point was, she should have said *something*.

He didn't know if that knowledge would have changed anything that had happened between them. But blast it, he'd had a right to know. He wasn't exactly in the habit of initiating virgins.

She abandoned her relaxed pose and sat up cross-legged on the bed. A position which did nothing to quiet the desire still quickening inside him.

Rick swallowed a groan and tried to keep his mind on the matter at hand.

"How did you know?" she asked, concern plain on her features. "Did I do something wrong?"

Wrong? Hell, no. He'd never had sex—no, he mentally corrected—that hadn't been just sex. He'd never *made love* like that before. He'd never felt every touch so deeply. Every sigh so softly. And while *she* might have been a virgin up until a few minutes ago, Rick had plenty of experiences to compare this one to.

And all of them came up short.

Because none of those experiences had involved his heart.

But he wasn't going to share that little piece of news. "I just knew, all right?" He came to a stop at the foot of the bed and stared down at her. "But you should have told me."

She shrugged.

He snapped. "How in the hell does a twenty-eight-year-old woman get to be a *virgin* for Pete's sake?" How could Tracy look like she did and be as fun and alluring and tempting and still be as pure as the proverbial driven snow? What the hell was the matter with the men she knew? Were they blind? Or just stupid?

"Forgive me," she said, her tone dripping with outraged sarcasm. Scooting off the bed, she faced him on her own two feet. "If I'd known you were going to be so picky, I could have spent a few nights trolling the docks looking for men to practice on."

"That's not what I meant, damn it!" He shoved one hand through his short hair.

"What exactly do you mean then, Rick?"

Even he didn't know the answer to that anymore.

She started pacing, her short, quick steps

taking her to the sliding glass doors and back again.

Watching the curve of her behind didn't help him any.

When she stopped in front of him, she leaned forward, hands on naked hips. He deliberately kept his gaze from locking onto her breasts.

"Do virgins scare the big, bad Marine?" she asked. "Is that it? Well relax then, because thanks to you, I am no longer in their number."

Count to ten, he told himself. Count to ten. He managed to get to two.

"Virgins don't scare me, lady," he growled, in a tone that his subordinates at the base had learned to fear and respect, "but you sure as hell do."

She drew her head back and grinned at him. "I think I'll take that as a compliment."

Figures. "You should have told me, Tracy."

"If I had told you, you might have

stopped." Smiling up at him, she added, "And I didn't want you to."

That should have made him feel better. It didn't.

"I don't know what you're so mad about." She shook her index finger at him like some old-maid schoolteacher. "If anybody's got the right to be upset here, it's me."

"I know that," he said tightly.

"You took a perfectly wonderful experience and turned it into a fight."

He reached up and pushed both hands through his hair, more to keep from reaching for her than anything else. She was right, in a way. What they'd shared had touched him deeper than he'd thought possible. But he knew damn well she hadn't yet considered the possible ramifications.

He had. In fact, those possibilities were scrambling through his mind now at lightning speed. How could he have been so stupid? So careless? It wasn't as if he was some teenager with more hormones than brains.

He was a *Marine,* for heaven's sake. If he

went into battle as unprepared as he'd faced tonight's little skirmish, he'd be a dead man.

On that pleasant thought, he stared down at her and tried to keep his voice steady as he asked, "Okay, Miss Feeling Wonderful...here's a question for you. Are you taking birth control pills?"

"As you just pointed out, I am—*was*—a virgin. Why would I need the pill?"

A sinking sensation opened up inside him, like a Black Hole sucking all life into its center. Tracy just stared at him, still blissfully unaware. But it would come to her, he told himself. Shouldn't take long, her being such a bloody genius and all. So he'd just wait and watch the truth hit her.

A moment later, his patience was rewarded.

Her eyes went wide and round. Her mouth dropped open. Her knees gave out and she plopped down to sit on the edge of the mattress.

"Still feeling wonderful?" he asked.

Eight

"**B**ingo!" he said softly.

From behind the hand covering her mouth, Tracy asked, "And you didn't use…?"

"No, I didn't," he said and started pacing again. Tracy watched him, but without her glasses he was so blurry she couldn't see anything interesting. At that thought, she felt a slow flush crowd her cheeks.

"My fault. Stupid," he muttered. "Didn't think. *Couldn't* think." He shook his head as he walked as if arguing with himself. "No excuse, damn it."

"You're not helping," she told him and had the satisfaction of seeing his blurry shape stop directly in front of her.

"There is no help to be had here, Tracy."

"This is as much my fault as yours," she said, trying to mentally sift through all of the careening thoughts ricocheting across her mind. But it was a wonder she could think at all so soon after the brain-numbing sensations she'd just experienced. Her body still humming with released energy, she mumbled, "I didn't even consider..."

"Yeah," he muttered and flopped down onto the mattress beside her. "I know."

Had what they'd shared affected him as deeply as it had her? She hugged that notion to her heart briefly before dismissing it. Why should he have been as staggered as she? *He* hadn't been a virgin, unprepared and startled by the final realization of a lifetime's worth of fantasies.

But if that were true, why was he so swept away he hadn't thought of protection, either?

Politely, she turned her head toward him

even if she couldn't see him. "I am curious," she said. "Don't you carry condoms around with you?"

Impossible to judge his expression, but from the tone of his voice, she didn't guess it was pleasant. "Contrary to what this might look like," he said, his voice low and dangerous, "I'm not a roving stud looking for conquests. I haven't carried condoms in my wallet since I was eighteen and hoping to get lucky."

In an odd sort of way, that made her feel better. At least she knew...what? That he hadn't thought he'd need a condom around her? Oh my, yes, that was just dandy.

"I thought Marines were supposed to be always prepared."

"That's the Boy Scouts."

"Oh."

An uncomfortable silence stretched out between them for what seemed a small eternity but was really only a few seconds. In that brief flash of time, Tracy considered the small possibility that she might be pregnant.

Along with the expected feelings of worry, anxiety and regret for behaving so stupidly came a small trickle of excitement.

She'd long ago given up any thoughts of having children of her own. After all, she was twenty-eight years old and not exactly a man magnet. And though the thought of being a single mother was a sobering one, her long-dormant maternal instincts were kicking up their heels and shouting ''yippee''!

Then her stomach twisted nervously and Tracy stood up, and carefully felt her way around the edge of the mattress. Reaching out, her fingers fumbled for her purse, then delved inside for her glasses. Putting them on, she turned to look at Rick.

Her breath caught in her throat and momentarily, she told herself she might have been better off to remain blind until this conversation was finished. Still sitting on the edge of the mattress, he could have been a model for an ancient Greek statue. Something called ''Incredible Male'' would be just about right.

Looking at miles of sun-browned skin and

muscles upon muscles did strange things to her already unsteady equilibrium. Especially since she could now admit, if only to herself, that she was in love with Rick Bennet. Hopelessly, stupidly in love.

God help her, she always had been.

Swallowing hard, she cleared her throat and tried to sound normal. "It won't do us any good to sit here worrying about what's already done."

He shot her a glance that told her he thought she was nuts. "So we're supposed to just forget about it?"

She couldn't have done that if her life depended on it. Tracy had the distinct impression that this night with Rick would be emblazoned in capital letters across her heart and mind for the rest of eternity. Even if it turned out, as she expected it would, that she wasn't pregnant. Oh, yeah, she told herself. She had it bad.

But she would spare herself the humiliation of Rick knowing that particular secret.

Forcing a smile, she folded her hands at her

waist and had only a moment to think how weird it was to be having this conversation while completely naked. Of course, if they hadn't been completely naked, this conversation wouldn't be necessary.

"All I'm saying is that everything will probably be fine." She smiled again, putting more determination behind the effort even as she reluctantly let go of her dream baby. "It was only the one time."

Planting his hands on his knees, he pushed himself off the bed. Scooping up his clothes from the floor, he tugged his jeans on and headed for the sliding glass door. Before leaving for his own room, he half-turned and locked his gaze with hers. "I wonder," he said thoughtfully, "just how many couples over the centuries have tried to console themselves with those particular words."

Early the next morning, Rick carried two cups of coffee back from the manager's office. Not that he needed caffeine to wake him up.

Hell, he hadn't slept all night. How could a man sleep after doing something so stupid?

So heart-stoppingly perfect.

His fingers tightened around the paper cups and he had to force himself to relax before he squeezed hard enough to crumple them.

Hours, he'd lain awake in the dark, reliving every moment with Tracy. Her touch. Her sighs. Damn it, he'd never felt so close to a woman before. One night with Tracy had made everything in his life up to that point seem meaningless. Trivial.

He'd wracked his brain trying to figure out what in the hell had happened between them and he was still no closer to an answer. She'd blindsided him without even trying. If anyone had told him a week ago that he would be in this position, he'd have laughed himself sick.

Rick Bennet? Master of the love 'em and leave 'em game, caught off-guard by a blond, freckled, nearly-blind pixie of a woman?

Most of his adult life, he'd told himself that he was a bad bet as husband material. That the military way of life was too hard on marriages. And that *those* were the reasons for his remaining single all these years. But, he wondered now, what if the real reason was that he'd simply never found the right woman? A woman he was willing to risk everything for. A woman who made him think about things like a home. Kids.

Kids?

Good grief. What if Tracy was pregnant?

Him? A father?

Don't think about that yet, the told himself. Maybe she was right. Maybe everything would turn out fine and they could simply walk away from each other as though this road trip had never happened.

Strange, but that idea didn't bring the flood of relief he might have expected.

He stopped dead on the wooden walkway and let his head fall back on his neck. Instantly, images of Tracy rose up in his already tortured mind. The way the wind caught her hair. The way she squinted when she refused to wear her glasses or contacts. Her laughter. Her touch. Her sighs. She'd really gotten to him. How did she tug on corners of his heart he hadn't known existed?

And what in the hell was he going to do about it?

Sighing heavily, he straightened up and headed for her room again. Best just to prime her with coffee, load her into the car and get to Oregon as fast as possible.

As he came around the corner, he saw her already up and dressed, standing at the edge of the deck, staring out at the ocean. Her short, blond curls danced gently in the soft sea wind. The turtlenecked, deep-blue sweater she wore over baby-blue slacks looked incredibly good on her. As she turned her head at the sound of his approach, he noticed that her sweater made the color of her eyes an impossibly beautiful blue.

A desperate, driving need for her slammed into his gut and left his knees shaking. Calling on every ounce of the strength and control he'd always prided himself on, he pushed the raging desire pulsing inside him aside and marched toward her as if he was on the parade grounds.

"Good morning," she said as he walked close enough to offer the coffee.

"Is it?" he asked bluntly, still battling the ferocious urge to grab her and wrap himself around her. Studying her features, he looked for the signs of sleeplessness he knew were etched into his own face. He didn't find them. Apparently, she'd had no trouble sleeping.

Damned if she didn't smile as she took a sip of coffee. Turning her head back to look at the view, she said softly, "I think so."

"Tracy…"

She shook her head, but still didn't look at him. "If you're going to apologize, I want to remind you that I'm not a morning person and I might take it badly."

"I'll take my chances." He studied her profile and saw her wince behind her glasses. "Damn it, Tracy, what am I supposed to say?"

"Why do you have to say anything?" she countered, finally half-turning her head to glance at him. She took another sip before adding, "We're two adults who enjoyed each other's company for a while."

Was that all it was? That spectacular coming together they'd shared? No, he told himself. It was more. Much more and they both knew it. He scowled darkly and took a swallow of coffee to keep from saying something he'd probably regret.

"Stop looking so fierce," she said on a short laugh. "It's not like I'm going to tell your mother on you or something."

"She's making jokes," he muttered to himself. He'd been up all night and she'd not only slept like a baby, but was kidding around about something that had shaken him to the bone.

Was this some sort of cosmic justice? Was Fate paying him back for all the times he'd taken a relationship too lightly?

"Besides," Tracy said, interrupting his thoughts as she turned around to face him, "I should be thanking you."

"What?" Would she *never* stop surprising him?

"Sure." She reached up to push her hair back from her face only to have the wind toss it across her eyes again. "Now that I'm... experienced, shall we say, I should be able to make my relationship with Brad sound all the more real."

"Brad?" He wasn't sure how he'd managed to squeeze that word past the hard knot in his throat. His gaze locked on the diamond ring from her pretend boyfriend and even he was surprised by the urge to rip it off her hand and toss it into the ocean.

"My fiancé?" she reminded him. "When I talk about him now, I should be able to convince anyone."

A bubble of something unpleasant started in the pit of his stomach. He wasn't sure whether to be pleased or insulted. She was going to use their night together as fodder for her imaginary stud?

Damn. He had felt the earth move, and she

was plotting a fictional romance.

Oh yeah. Karma was lots of fun.

Crossing the state line into Oregon, Tracy started to feel the first twinges of misgiving. She shot a look at her companion and wasn't in the least surprised to find his face still set in the same dark and stormy mask he'd worn all morning.

She turned her head and stared out at the passing scenery instead. Thick stands of forest lined the highway, and for the first time in her life, she wasn't moved by the sight. Not even the redwoods were enough of a distraction.

Soon they'd be home. Juneport. Surrounded by friends and families. Swept up into the whole reunion thing. And this little…interlude would be over.

Disappointment and regret simmered in her stomach and sent out long tentacles to reach up and grab her heart.

She was going to miss Rick. Miss being alone with him. Joking and laughing with him. Making love with him.

Her eyes squeezed shut on the thought and

once again, images of the night before filled her mind. She couldn't stop thinking about it. Couldn't stop reliving every touch. Every whisper.

Suddenly good old Brad seemed like chopped liver. How could her made-up Marine ever compare to the real thing? And how could she pretend to love a Marine who wasn't the *right* Marine?

She couldn't.

"You know," she said abruptly, "I've been thinking."

"What?" he asked as if he really didn't want to know, he was just being polite.

She turned to look at him. "About Brad…"

His features tightened.

She went on anyway. "I've decided that instead of a Marine, I'm going to make him an accountant."

"You're thinking about *him?*"

"Well, yeah." Better she occupy her mind with a fictional man that the one who looked like he could chew right through the steering wheel. "We're almost home. So I thought we should have our stories straight."

"I don't think it's a good idea," he grumbled, his jaw twitching spasmodically.

Tracy stiffened slightly in her seat. "I didn't ask for your opinion. I simply thought you'd like to know what story I'm going to tell before I tell it."

His jaw worked furiously for a moment or two. "It won't work," he said finally.

"Oh, really? And why's that?"

He shot her a look from behind those damned dark glasses of his.

"For one, because Brad's a wimp and nobody's going to be impressed with a bean counter."

"He's not a wimp."

"He's no Marine."

"He's a very successful accountant," she snapped.

"A *prize* wimp."

"This really isn't any of your business, you know," she pointed out.

"It should be."

Tracy frowned at him. The conversation was confusing, but at least it was conversation. "What do you mean?"

"I'll be Brad," he said.

Okay, now he'd gone beyond confusing and straight into the Twilight Zone. She stared at him for a long moment before pointing out, very reasonably she thought, "You can't be Brad. Everyone in town knows you!"

He sucked in a long gulp of air, then reached up and pulled his sunglasses off. Glancing at her, he explained, "I meant, I'll pretend to be your fiancé. Then we can lose *Brad* entirely."

Her body reacted to his idea with an excited shiver. Instantly, visions of a weekend spent in Rick's company danced in her mind. She thought of the kisses and cuddling she could expect from her real live fiancé. Just by agreeing to his outlandish idea, Tracy would gain a few more days of a rich, full fantasy life— one where Rick Bennet loved her.

Her eyes misted over at the thought, but she blinked away the moisture and forced herself back to reality with a grinding halt. If she indulged in that much fantasy, going back to a life without him would be even more painful than it was already going to be.

"No way." She shook her head firmly. "Not a chance."

"Why not?" he demanded. "Like you said, everyone in town knows me. A real live fiancé is much easier to believe in than a conspicuously absent one."

"This is nuts." A part of her longed to play along. Pretend that she and Rick were engaged. That he had given her the ring on her finger along with promises of a love-filled future. But the still-rational Tracy folded her arms across her chest and shook her head. "Completely nuts."

"And an imaginary playmate isn't?"

Gritting her teeth, she said, "You didn't think it was nuts a couple of days ago. Why now, when we're less than an hour from home?" Turning her head to look at him, she added, "You've hardly said a word to me all morning and now you volunteer to be my fiancé? Why?''

His grip on the steering wheel flexed and relaxed several times before he answered. ''An in-the-flesh Marine Captain is better than a made-up accountant, right?''

If the Marine Captain was *him,* Tracy thought, he was better than just about anybody. But all she said was, ''I suppose.''

''Gee, thanks.'' A brief, half smile caught at the corner of his mouth. ''But that's not the only reason.''

''Then what?''

Rick's smile evaporated. ''Think about it, Trace. You can't ignore the possibility that you might be pregnant.''

''I won't be.''

''I don't think the power of positive thinking has a lot to do with the outcome of this particular situation,'' Rick grumbled, forcing himself to keep his eyes on the road. He'd been doing plenty of thinking this morning and had finally come up with this idea. It was the only workable solution.

"It can't hurt," she said, tightening her arms over her chest in what could only be a defensive maneuver.

"And neither can this," he said flatly. "If you *are* pregnant, Tracy, are you going to tell your folks that Brad is the father?"

He shot her a quick glance and saw her wince as reality reared its ugly head. While he had her full attention, he went on quickly. "Your baby can't have a pretend father. Even if you go ahead with your plan to 'break up' with the guy in a month or so, your folks will expect to run into Brad at some point over the years since he'll have joint custody of your child."

"Oh..."

And he would be damned if he'd have *anybody* thinking that *his* baby had been fathered by the fictional accountant.

"I figure," he said, "we announce our engagement. You can still 'break up' with me if you're not pregnant."

She turned her head to look at him. "And if I am?"

If she was, then there'd be no breaking up. He'd see to it. Still, he sensed now might not be the time to tell her that. He inhaled sharply, deeply. "We'll worry about that when the time comes."

"I don't know..." she said, shaking her head as she thought about the whole thing.

"It makes sense, Tracy."

"Maybe."

And, he thought, his idea had the added bonus of ensuring that he wouldn't have to listen to Tracy rave about "Brad" for the whole reunion weekend. He really hated that guy.

Not to mention the fact that he wouldn't have the slightest bit of trouble convincing anyone that he and Tracy were an item. Hell, just sitting beside her in the car was enough to make him want to find the nearest motel.

"And what do we tell our families?" she asked.

That question hit him like a cold shower. Rick scowled thoughtfully. He hadn't thought about them.

"Shouldn't we tell *them* the truth at least?"

"This just keeps getting more and more complicated," he muttered. Driving home had seemed like such a good idea at the time. A few days to himself. To think about his life—where he'd been and where he was headed. Now, he was more confused than ever.

"Tell me about it," she said with feeling.

"Okay," Rick said, nodding to himself. "We tell them the truth, since they probably wouldn't believe the lie anyway."

Tracy sniffed. "Well, thank you very much."

Rick bit back a groan of disgust. All he'd meant was his parents had given up on him ever getting married. But judging from the tilt of Tracy's chin and the set of her jaw, she hadn't taken his statement that way at all.

Just like a real couple, he told himself.

They pulled up in front of Tracy's parents' house an hour later. Rick set the brake and turned the engine off before looking at her. "You ready?"

Tracy tore her gaze from the blue-and-white

two-storied Victorian house to glance at him. He had his Marine face on. Firm jaw, steely eyes, full lips thinned into a grim slash.

Oh, yeah. The very picture of a happy groom-to-be.

But then again, she probably didn't look much better. Strange, but when she'd come up with this plan to invent Brad, it had all seemed so simple.

How had everything come so unravelled in such a short period of time?

"I guess so," she said. "We might as well..."

"Tracy!"

Her sister's shout interrupted her and Tracy turned in her seat to watch Meg already running toward the car. Right behind her came the older Halls and Bennets. Apparently, they'd all gathered together for a homecoming.

A flutter of excitement rose up inside Tracy and for the moment, she forgot about everything else in the pleasure of being with her family again.

She opened the car door, jumped out and ran across the grass toward her sister. The toe of her shoe hit an automatic sprinkler head. Eyes wide, she stumbled and would have fallen flat on her face, if Meg hadn't been there to grab her.

Laughing, her older sister said, "Well, you're dressed better than the last time I saw you, but you haven't really changed much, have you? Still tripping on everything in sight."

"Guess so," Tracy said, glancing down to see if she'd broken her foot or just acquired another stunning bruise. "When did Dad install..."

"Ohmigod!" Meg shrieked, grabbing Tracy's left hand in an iron grip and staring down at the diamond winking at her in the sunlight. "You're *engaged!* And you didn't tell me! Who to?"

Tracy inhaled sharply. Trust Meg to spot that ring almost instantly. She looked beyond her sister's shoulder and saw her mother's face light up with excitement. Oh, dear.

Rick stepped up to them at just that moment and Tracy looked up at him helplessly. Silently, her eyes demanded that he say something.

"Ohmigod!" Meg yelled again, as she watched the two of them for a split second. She half turned to shout to their parents. "You'll never believe it! Rick and Tracy are engaged!"

Tracy gasped and glanced from her sister to her mother, to Rick's mom. All three women were grinning. Oh, for heaven's sake!

"Meg," Tracy grabbed at her sister and tried to speak over the uproar. But Meg shrugged her off and her voice was lost in an excited babble of voices.

Their parents surrounded them on the front yard, everyone talking at once.

"It's about time," Dave Hall said as he pumped Rick's hand enthusiastically.

Tracy stared at her father. "Daddy..."

"Damn straight," Bill Bennet added and slapped his son on the back hard enough to stagger him.

"Look, Dad..." Rick said.

No one was listening.

"I thought they'd *never* see how perfect they are for each other," Patty Bennet said and hugged her son fiercely before giving Tracy a kiss on each cheek and a proud, motherly smile.

Nancy Hall pushed her friend out of the way and clasped her youngest daughter to her breast. Tracy looked up at Rick as her mother said through her tears, "I'm just so happy."

Nine

———

"**I** can't believe you guys were dating and you didn't tell me," Meg said, then scowled at Rick playfully. "And you let me think you were doing me a favor by giving her a ride to the reunion."

Tracy's head was spinning. No. Maybe it was the world that was spinning. She shot a look at Rick as he dropped one arm across her shoulders.

"Just how long has this been going on between you two?" Meg asked no one in particular.

Her voice sounded as though it was coming from far, far away. In fact, over the buzzing in her ears, Tracy was having a hard time hearing any of the excited voices bubbling around her. Frowning, she shook her head to clear it and tried to concentrate.

It was all so weird. Glancing at the familiar faces surrounding them, Tracy tried to see some signs that they were all playing a joke. But her mother's blue eyes were still damp with tears and Patty Bennet kept looking at Rick as though her son had just won the Nobel Prize or something. Their dads stood beaming at them proudly and Meg couldn't seem to stand still. She kept hopping from foot to foot in her excitement.

"Wait'll I get home and tell John," she said, reaching out to give Tracy's hand a quick squeeze.

"We just knew it," Rick's mother said, grinning at Tracy's mom. "We knew that if the two of you ever spent any time together at all, you'd realize what we've always known."

Nancy Hall kissed her daughter, glanced at Rick, wiped the tears from her cheeks and finished her friend's statement. "That you're so perfect for each other."

Huh? The Nerd and Mr. Wonderful—perfect for each other?

Rick pressed her up against him and she was grateful for the support. Otherwise, she might have toppled over.

Tracy opened her mouth and felt her throat work, but no sound came out. She snapped her jaw shut again as her sister continued talking.

"This is just so cool," she practically cooed, looking at Rick and Tracy as if she was their fairy godmother. "So, when's the wedding?"

Everyone stopped talking at once. A dog barked somewhere along the street and the hollow, roaring sound of a nearby skateboard drifted on the chill air.

Tracy stared into five pairs of interested eyes. Her family. People she loved. She swallowed heavily around a surprisingly large knot in her throat. How was she supposed to lie to

these people? How had she ever imagined she
could lie to them?

She slumped against Rick as she stared finally into her mother's teary eyes. The truth
crowded her soul. Confession hovered on her
lips.

Then Rick said, ''We haven't decided yet.''

The spell was broken and the excited voices
started up again.

''Fall, then,'' Patty Bennet said decisively.

''Or winter,'' Nancy Hall muttered, tapping
her chin as she thought about it.

''I think spring would be perfect,'' Meg
threw in as she joined the two other women
walking back toward the house. ''By then this
baby will be born, and I could buy a new dress
that isn't sized like a tent.''

The simple little lie swelled to amazing proportions. Every instinct she possessed
screamed at Tracy to stop them. Confess.
Bring this whole embarrassing episode to a
halt before it went any further. She didn't
even have to stay for the stupid reunion. Instead, she could swallow her Dramamine,

catch the first train out of town, go home and hide until the embarrassment of this moment faded away. Shouldn't take more than ten or twenty years.

She took a half step to follow after them, but Rick's grip on her shoulders tightened, pinning her to him.

With one last slap of congratulations on Rick's back, their fathers moved off in the direction of the garage, clearly trying to avoid rabid wedding discussions.

"I don't believe this," Tracy muttered when they were alone again.

"Pretty strange," Rick agreed.

His arm still lay across her shoulders, and Tracy felt the hard, solid strength of him pressing along her side. Briefly, she let herself enjoy the sensation of being that close to him again. But then the magnitude of what had just happened settled down on her.

"We have to go talk to them. Our moms. In another hour, they'll have the church booked and the cake ordered."

He stared off after their mothers as if he

still couldn't believe what had just happened. Idly, he moved his hand up and down her arm, igniting her bloodstream and shifting her concern from the lie that had swallowed them to the flickers of desire touching every inch of her body with fiery fingers.

After a long moment, he shifted his gaze to hers. "Maybe we should just leave it alone."

"We can't do that," she argued, trying to concentrate despite losing herself in the green of his eyes. "We agreed to tell them the truth."

"Yeah," he said, and turned her around to face him. "I know." He wrapped both arms around her and pulled her close. Looking down into her eyes he said, "But look at it this way—with our mothers talking, the word will spread all over town."

"True." And that was what she'd wanted, wasn't it? To come back home a changed woman? Elegant, beautiful, successful, with a loving fiancé in tow?

His hands splayed against her back, dragging her even closer. Her breathing quickened as he pressed her body to his. A now-familiar ache throbbed into life. Sunshine filtered through the leaves in the oak that shaded the yard and dusted his face with fluttering shadows. His green eyes glittered. His arms tightened around her until she thought her ribs would snap and her lungs collapse.

And if he would just go on holding her, she wouldn't mind so much.

"Rick," she said, her voice coming out in a hushed whisper of sound.

"Yeah?" His gaze moved over her features slowly as he lowered his head to hers.

Oh, my.

She tipped her head back, already moving to meet him even as she said, "Neighbors might be watching..."

One of his hands snaked up her back to cup her head, his fingers threading through her hair. "Let 'em watch," he murmured just before his lips claimed hers. "We're engaged. Right?"

Here it was. The last chance to call for reason. She could step back away from him now.

March into the house and set their parents and Meg straight. Or...she could be engaged. For a long weekend, she could live out her fantasy of being the woman Rick Bennet loved.

He paused just a breath away from her mouth and asked again, "Right?"

"Right," she said on a sigh and let his kiss splinter her thoughts.

Rick walked into his old bedroom in his parents' house and found it pretty much the same as the day he'd left it.

He tossed the duffel bag onto the narrow bed, stood in the center of the room and did a slow turn, letting his gaze sweep over the remnants of his childhood.

A red-and-white pennant from the last big game of his senior year of high school was still tacked to the wall. A Marine Corps recruiting poster hung alongside it. Two footballs and a flat basketball were piled into a corner near a trunk that he would be willing to bet still contained schoolbooks and outgrown clothes. His mother, the pack rat, never threw away a thing.

Smiling to himself, he crossed the room to the mirror above his old dresser. Photographs tucked into the frame stared back at him. He and his brothers standing beside Andy's wreck of a car. Meg in her prom dress. Meg, Tracy and his brothers on the beach that last spring before the end of high school.

He looked at Meg's smiling, young face and tried to remember the searing love he'd thought would last forever. But it wouldn't come. Frowning, his gaze slipped past her to the younger girl in the background.

Tracy. Barefoot, wearing shorts and an old tee shirt, her hair was in a ponytail and she was grinning so broadly at Andy, Rick could plainly see her braces.

His heartbeat staggered.

He sucked in a breath of air and leaned closer to the photo. Sure, she'd grown up. Now she looked sleek and sophisticated, her clothes picture perfect, but that smile remained the same. And carried enough strength to knock the breath out of his lungs.

"Good grief!" he muttered and reached up to shove one hand through his hair.

"I'm so glad you decided to stay here with us," her mother said as she helped Tracy carry her luggage into her old room.

Smiling, Tracy dropped a bag onto her bed, then turned to take the suitcase from her mom. "Where else would I stay?"

Nancy Hall smoothed her graying blond hair unnecessarily and studied her younger daughter for a long moment before saying, "At a hotel, I guess. With Rick."

"Oh." Keep it up, Tracy, she told herself. Remember the game.

"I mean, well..." Her mother actually blushed before finishing, "Not that I'd *approve,* of course, but you are engaged after all. I'd understand if you..."

"No, really Mom," she said quickly, too quickly if her mother's startled expression was anything to judge by. "Rick and I talked about it. We both decided we'd like to spend time with our families.''

Nancy Hall smiled and nodded. ''Good. Besides, he's only three doors down. I'm sure you'll still see plenty of each other. Heaven knows, when he and Meg were an item, he was here all the...'' she broke off.

''It's okay, Mom,'' Tracy told her with a sigh. ''I lived here then too, remember?''

''Of course,'' she said and shook her head. ''It's all water under the bridge, isn't it? You were all so young then...''

Tracy knew the signs and spotted the tears filling her mother's eyes. She crossed the room and wrapped her mom in a hug. ''Don't cry,'' she said.

Patting her daughter, Nancy sniffed, then stepped back, moving toward the door. ''I'm just being silly, I know. It's just that, well, my baby's getting married.''

Tracy felt the knife of betrayal stab deep in her chest and twist itself around mercilessly.

''I'm so happy for you, Sweetie,'' her mom said with another sniff. ''You have everything you ever wanted. A good job, a home of your own, and now, Rick.''

"Yeah," Tracy said softly. "Everything I ever wanted."

"Are you all right?"

"Huh?" She nodded quickly. "Oh, sure. Just tired, I guess. It was a long trip."

"I'll let you get some rest before dinner, then." Her mother moved to the door and laid one hand on the brass knob. Glancing back over her shoulder, she let her gaze drift over her younger daughter. "You really look wonderful, Tracy. Love suits you."

Then she left, still smiling, and closed the door behind her.

Love suited her.

She couldn't help wondering what she'd look like when she was alone again. Would the pretty new clothes, cosmetic makeover and trendy haircut make the slightest amount of difference? Or would she turn into a pumpkin at the end of reunion weekend?

Tracy turned and walked across the room to the wide, padded windowseat where over the years she'd spent so many hours day-dreaming. Outside, the first stars were already flickering to life in the darkening night.

Slumping down onto the rose-patterned cushion, she stared out at the street where she'd grown up, but she wasn't seeing the familiar houses or the neatly trimmed lawns. Instead, her mind conjured Rick's image, and she tried to tell herself that a weekend with him would be enough to ease the long, empty years stretching out ahead of her.

Midnight and he couldn't sleep.

Maybe it was being back in his boyhood room, surrounded by remnants of his past. And maybe it was remembering how he'd spent the night before, wrapped in Tracy's arms, buried deep within her.

His body tightened uncomfortably, and he groaned before vaulting out of the bed and grabbing up his jeans from the nearby chair. He needed to walk. To move. To feel the night air on his face.

He should never have agreed to attend the

reunion. He should have stayed on base, he told himself. Back at Pendleton, things were simple. Black and white. He had his duties to perform and he did them.

Rick liked things neat. He preferred clearly defined lines. He had a road map for his life all neatly plotted out. So what was this weekend? he asked himself.

A detour?

Or something more serious...more long-lasting?

Buttoning up his worn, battered jeans, he considered that last thought, then instinctively veered away from it again. Catching himself, he forced that thought back into his brain and tried to study it objectively as snatches of conversations with Tracy filtered through his mind.

She'd made him remember that his family had thrived on military bases. His parents' marriage hadn't gone under; it had gotten stronger. Then he thought of the couples he knew back at the base. And for the first time, he honestly admitted to the twinges of jealousy he'd felt when his friends hurried home to their wives…and he went home to the TV.

A hollow, empty feeling opened up inside him as he realized just how little he really *had* in his life. A satisfying career and good friends, yes. Someone who gave a damn whether or not he came home at night, no.

Mind racing, body tight and humming with an excess of energy, Rick stomped into his shoes, drew a T-shirt over his head and snatched up his jacket as he slipped out his door into the dimly lit hallway. Tossing a quick glance down the hall to his parents' closed door, he made a sharp right and headed for the stairs.

The Bennet boys had learned long ago which steps were the squeaky ones. Deftly, he avoided them and let himself out of the house as quietly as possible.

Suburban silence greeted him.

The night air was cold and damp. Long strings of clouds chased each other across the night sky, skimming over the half moon and bathing the world in shadows. A light film of fog drifted in from the ocean, twisting in the wind like ghostly fingers.

Shrugging deeper into the folds of his jacket, Rick stepped off the porch and crossed the yard to the street. Deliberately, he turned in the opposite direction from the house where Tracy was no doubt sleeping soundly.

Grumbling under his breath, he started walking down the narrow, tree-lined street. Memories assailed him, and his mind swam with images that scuttled one after the other through his brain. And damned if every last one of them wasn't of the last three days.

He stopped in the middle of the street and whirled around to glare at the Hall house, an almost shapeless blur half hidden in fog. Somehow, in three short days, Tracy had wormed her way under his skin. He couldn't draw a breath without thinking of her. He couldn't sleep without dreaming of her.

Before he could talk himself out of it, he was headed for her house. Slipping across the yard, he remembered the times he'd sneaked out at night to see Meg, but somehow he couldn't recall experiencing the same sense of urgency that rode him now.

He simply had to see Tracy.

Bending down, he picked up a few small pebbles from Mrs. Hall's flower bed, then stepped back and tossed a couple of them at the darkened second-story window he knew to be hers.

The tinkle of sound seemed overly loud to him, but no light came on in response, so he tossed a few more, wincing as they made contact with the glass.

A moment later, a soft yellow glow rose up from behind the white lace sheers. Rick's gaze locked on the window, and when Tracy appeared, pushing the curtains aside and shoving the window open, he pulled in his first easy breath in an hour.

"Rick?" She leaned out, and set her glasses on her nose. Her voice whispered down to him, "What are you doing?"

He smiled to himself. She wore a plain white nightgown and her curly hair was pulled back into a short ponytail. She looked young and beautiful and completely Tracy. Desire twisted in his gut, squeezing the air from his lungs. And something deeper, richer, cloaked his heart.

"Come downstairs," he said, his voice tight and low.

"Now?"

He laughed shortly. "Yes, now."

She shook her head, but said, "Just a minute." Then she closed her window and turned away.

Rick was already moving toward the front porch. Silently, he remembered the last time he'd been at this house in the middle of the night. He and Meg had dissolved their elopement. Now he was back years later, and waiting for Meg's sister filled him with an eagerness he'd never known before.

He took the four short steps to the porch in two strides and was waiting when she opened the door.

"Is everything all right?" she asked, as he took her arm and guided her to the shadow-filled, fog-draped, far end of the porch.

"Fine," he said and eased down onto the wooden slat swing, bringing her down beside him. She shivered and he wrapped his arms around her.

"What are you doing here in the middle of the night?" she asked, cuddling into him, he hoped for more than warmth.

"I just..." What? Couldn't sleep because thoughts of you kept crowding my mind? No. He was having a hard enough time admitting that to himself, let alone to Tracy. Sliding his hands up and down her back, he lied quietly, "I'm making our engagement look good. Our folks probably expect us to do a little sneaking out for some quiet time together."

"Oh," she said, and inched closer to him on the swing.

"Cold?"

"A little," she admitted and smiled at him. "I should have put my robe on."

He was glad she hadn't. The simple, white cotton nightgown was the furthest thing from erotic he'd ever seen. Yet somehow, on Tracy, it was more sexy than the slinkiest black lace could ever be.

The quick, hot stirring of passion rippled through him, and his breath caught at the force of it. This was why he'd come here tonight. He'd relived every minute of their time together the night before, and Rick needed to know if what he'd felt was real—or just a reaction to the magic of that moment.

But it wasn't only desire driving him. It was a new and intoxicating feeling that terrified—and fascinated—him.

"Kiss me, Tracy," he murmured, and her breath quickened.

He slid one hand up to caress the length of her neck and he felt the staccato pulse beat at the base of her throat.

"Rick..."

A swirl of fog curled around them, blanketing them in a soft, damp mist. They were adrift in the gray-shrouded darkness, in a world cut off from everyone else.

She shivered again, but this time, Rick felt sure it wasn't from the cold. If she was feeling half what he was, she was burning up inside, being consumed by a fire that only seemed to grow brighter and hotter by the second.

He dipped his head, claimed her slightly parted lips and felt a sense of coming home. At the first brush of her mouth on his, his insides tightened like a coiled spring. She moved into him with a wordless sigh, wrapping her arms around his neck as he pulled her onto his lap.

Lifting his head, he stared down at her for a long moment. He had his answer, he told himself as he gently pulled her glasses off and, leaning to one side, set them on the floor beside them.

It was real. The feelings that swept through him when they kissed were real and overwhelming. She made him think of hearth and home. She made him want to find a dragon to slay for her. She made him want to be everything she'd ever needed.

He bent his head to hungrily take his fill of her mouth, her tongue, her lips. He couldn't get enough of her.

Need, desire, passion, rolled through him, like a Marine invasion. And on their heels came tenderness, gentleness, love. As he would in a military campaign, he responded with all of his forces. His hands moved over her body, she squirmed against him, rubbing her bottom over his already hard and aching groin.

Rick growled from deep in his throat and tipped her head back into the crook of his left arm. She tightened her grip on his neck and raised herself up high enough to press her breasts against his chest.

She moaned gently and he took the sound and the breath it had ridden on as his own. He wanted more, needed more.

Rick had never known such wild, uncontrollable desire before. Such a desperate need to connect with a woman. To claim her, body and soul. His heart pounded, his mind raced with possibilities and his body demanded some sort of release.

Still plundering the secrets of her mouth, he slid his right hand up, along the inside of her thighs to the very heart of her. She whimpered gently and shifted in his arms, turning toward him, even as her tongue swept along his in a slow dance of seduction.

The darkness shielded them. The fog enveloped them. Rick kept his mouth locked to hers, swallowing her moans, protecting their privacy as his fingers explored her.

Breathing labored, he pushed her higher and higher. He felt her heartbeat thundering as she pressed herself closer to him. Her hips bucked beneath his hand. She planted her feet on the old swing and lifted herself into his touch.

He wanted to take her further, deeper. He needed to touch her as deeply as she had him. His left arm tightened around her and when she tore her mouth from his to stare up at him through wide, passion-glazed eyes, it was all he could do to remember to breathe.

"This is crazy," she managed to say in a broken hush of sound.

It was. He knew it. In fact, the last three days had been crazy—and wonderful.

He gave her a strained, half smile. "Want me to stop?"

"*No*..." She shook her head from side to side and bit down hard on her bottom lip. "Don't stop. Don't ever stop."

"Never, Tracy," he whispered and dipped first one finger, then two into her depths. Slipping in and out of her warmth, he coaxed her along, urging her to find the satisfaction that would ease him as well as her. "Take it, honey," he said, his voice no more than a suggestion of sound.

Her breath staggered and her fingers clutched at his shoulders. "Rick..." she moaned gently, turning her face into his chest as her hips rocked rhythmically against his hand.

"Let go, honey," he said on a breath and held her tight as his thumb brushed across her most tender nubbin of flesh.

She gasped. Her inner muscles contracted and he felt the first quaking, rippling climax take her. Her body trembled. He tightened his grip on her as she buried her face in his chest, muffling her cries against him.

And when it was over and she lay quiet in his arms again, Rick smoothed her nightgown down and gathered her close. A sense of peace stole over him as he held her, feeling her heartbeat gradually slow to normal. Somehow, his own driving need had been satisfied in pleasuring her.

"I can't believe we just did that," she whispered a few minutes later.

He couldn't believe it either. A career Marine, making love to a woman on her front porch in the middle of the night where anyone might have seen...or heard them, no matter how dark it was or how quiet they'd tried to be.

And his only regret was that it was over.

"I'm not sorry," he said and looked down into her eyes.

"Neither am I," she told him softly.

In response, Rick's arms closed around her. He pressed his forehead to hers. Her rapid breathing was the only sound he heard.

Well, he'd wanted to know if it was real. Now he had his answer, though he wasn't sure what to do about it.

Apparently, this pretend engagement was taking on a life of its own.

Ten

___

She couldn't avoid seeing Rick even if she wanted to.

Which, despite the embarrassing memory of last night's scene on the porch swing, she didn't.

Still, Tracy thought as she stared through her sister's living-room window at Rick and her brother-in-law, she could have used a few hours' reprieve. Time to get her thoughts together. Time to think of a way to look at him without blushing like some idiot high-school kid.

But no. Rick had materialized on her front porch early this morning, ready to take her out to Meg and John's small farm. It was a short ride, though, and she'd babbled incoherently throughout the whole trip, never giving him a chance to refer to what they'd shared the night before.

A wave of fresh heat suddenly washed over her. In the bright light of day, it was almost impossible to believe she'd practically had sex on her parents' front porch.

She shivered at the memory and fought down the fiery tingles spreading through her body. What had happened to her in the last few days? She'd gone from being virginal to insatiable in less than a week.

"Hey," Meg said as she entered the room behind her, "can't you take your eyes off him for a minute?"

Tracy guiltily whipped around to face her older sister.

Meg carried a small, wooden tray bearing two steaming cups of coffee and two thick slices of chocolate cake. She set it down on the living-room table and plopped down onto the couch.

"Come on," she said, holding out one of the thick, yellow-and-white cups, "talk to me. You can stare at Rick for the rest of your life."

Or at least for the next few days, Tracy thought, but she dutifully walked to the couch and took a seat beside her sister.

As Meg launched into a monologue, Tracy looked around the clean, but incredibly cluttered room. Overstuffed chairs, the worn, flowered-fabric sofa, a fireplace whose mantel held framed photos of each of her nieces and nephews. Toys, dolls, shoes and socks dotted the surface of the blue-and-white braided oval covering most of the pine plank floor.

It was the image of a well-loved, well-lived-in, home.

If walls could talk, these would have told tales of kids and late-night hugs and shared secrets and lots of laughter.

Instantly, Tracy thought of her own condo. Sterile. Painfully neat. Unlived in. A surprising catch in her throat had her blinking back an unexpected sheen of tears.

And after this trip, it would seem even emptier.

"Are you okay?" Meg asked and laid one hand on her arm.

Shaken out of her reveries, Tracy nodded, sniffed and gave her sister a watery smile. "Sure," she assured her. "I'm fine." Then, trying for a shift in subject, she asked, "Where are the kids?"

Meg laughed. "Are you kidding? I chased them all off early this morning. They're at their friends' houses. I wanted some quiet time with you." She shook her head and sent her long blond hair flying back over her shoulders. "And trust me, with the 'Frantic Four' around, there *is* no quiet time."

The tiniest twinge of envy pierced Tracy's heart. Her older sister had a husband who adored her, a rapidly expanding family and a warm, cozy home. She, on the other hand, had a two-bedroom condo, a long list of business

associates and had had to make up a fiancé in
order to avoid pity.

Strange how two women raised in the same
house could have lives that turned out so differently. She couldn't help but wonder what
her life might have been like if she'd had just
a bit of Meg's self-confidence when she was
growing up.

Tracy tried to smile at her sister, but found
tears were closer than laughter. Quickly, she
spoke up. "Soon to be 'Frantic Five,'" she
pointed out and reached to lay the palm of her
hand against Meg's slightly bulged abdomen.

A quick twist of anxiety skittered through
her as she realized that she, too, might be
pregnant right now. And though a part of her
would love it to be true, she had to admit that
the chances were pretty slim.

"Yeah." Her sister's smile went soft and
dreamy. "Can you believe it? Another one."
She caught Tracy's eye and shrugged. "You
probably think I'm nuts," she allowed. "But
I just *love* babies."

"You're not nuts," Tracy went into defensive mode instinctively. "You're a terrific mother."

"I hope so," she said and laid her own hand protectively against the mound of her child.

Doubts? Tracy thought. Meg?

The other woman's gaze slanted toward the window, and the yard beyond where she knew her husband was. "John and I love kids, y'know. We'll have as many as God sends us. I just..."

"Just what?" Her own problems forgotten, Tracy scooted closer on the couch.

"It's silly," Meg confessed and set her coffee cup down onto the tray again before leaning back into the cushiony sofa. Shooting her sister a warning look, she said, "If you ever repeat any of this, I'll deny it—then find an affordable hit man."

A smile twitched at the corners of Tracy's mouth. She crossed her heart, then held up three fingers. "Solemn swear."

Meg nodded, satisfied. "Okay, then." She pulled in a deep breath and said, "I never told you this before, but I've always sort of…well, envied you.''

''What?'' She hadn't meant to laugh, but the very idea struck her as ludicrous. Meg had everything Tracy had ever wanted. And *she* envied *her?*

''Don't misunderstand,'' her big sister said quickly, holding up one hand as if in warning. ''I wouldn't change a thing about my life.'' She lifted her chin and idly stroked her hand over the arm of the couch. ''I'm crazy about John. Can't imagine a life without him. Or the kids. And living on a farm is perfect for me.''

''Then what…?'' Tracy didn't get it.

''Well,'' Meg curled one leg up underneath her and leaned toward her sister, ''every once in a while, when things are completely nuts around here, I think about you…*alone* in your house. Your own business. Clients who admire you.'' She laughed shortly. ''Able to go to the bathroom by yourself.''

''But,'' Tracy cut in, ''you have so much.''

''Don't I know it,'' her sister said. ''And

I'm grateful for all of it. But you know, Tracy, you have something I never did.''

What could *that* be?

''I was never any good at school. And you were always so smart.''

She felt the neon sign proclaiming *Nerd* flash onto her forehead.

''I know I never told you this,'' Meg confessed and reached out to catch her sister's hand. ''But I was as proud of you as Mom and Dad were. Still am.''

She looked into Meg's eyes and saw the truth there. A truth she'd never seen before. A new sheen of tears welled up in Tracy's eyes and she blinked furiously to keep them at bay. Her heart ached and a knot formed in her throat, almost cutting off her air.

Pride blossomed inside her and for the first time, she looked at her older sister and felt like her equal. Maybe old clichés became clichés because they were true. *The grass did look greener on the other side of the fence.*

After a long, comforting hug, Meg sat back, picked up her cake and dug in. Around a big bite, she asked, "So. Tell me all about you and Rick. When did you two start dating, and why didn't you tell me?"

Tracy's eyes widened at the abrupt shift in subject. Her spirits sank at the same rapid rate. Here they were, with her sister baring her soul, inviting confidences and now Tracy would be forced to lie to her.

"And," Meg whispered with a guilty glance around her as if to make sure they were still alone, "I want to know something else, too. Is he as good in bed as I always thought he would be?"

Heat flooded her face as explicit memories rushed through her mind. And along with those images, came another, very satisfying thought. Rick and Meg had never…she smiled to herself.

"Ooohh…" Meg leaned in, wiggling her eyebrows. "If even the thought of it can make you blush," she said, "I want details."

Rick handed John a wrench and leaned against the car fender as the other man dove beneath the hood again.

"So," his old friend said, his voice muffled and oddly echoing off the engine, "you and Tracy. Who would have guessed it?"

"Yeah," Rick said, frowning. He shot a glance at the farmhouse across the yard from them as if he could see through the walls to where Tracy sat with her sister.

He knew she'd tried to avoid him this morning. But then, that's why he'd planted himself on her parents' swing and waited for her until she came out. Of course, sitting on that swing would never be the same again.

Not after last night.

His fingers curled into fists at the memory. His breath strained in and out of his lungs. Over and over again, he'd relived that moment when she'd dissolved in his arms. When her climax had had her turning in to his chest to muffle her cries.

He wanted that again. He wanted to feel her heart beating just for him. He wanted her smiles. Her tears. Her love.

Love? Marriage?

Rick waited a beat for the familiar feeling of blind panic to set in and when it didn't come, he almost smiled. Could a man's life really change so dramatically in such a short period of time?

But would Tracy be happy with the nomadic life of a career soldier? Could what they shared survive?

"Would it work?" he muttered aloud.

"Of course it'll work," John said, clearly insulted. "The truck's a heap, I grant you, but I can always get it working again."

Rick shook his head and looked at his friend as the man straightened up. Thankfully, John had completely misconstrued what he'd been saying. "You always were a good hand with an engine," he said.

"No kidding!" John laughed and shoved his black hair out of his eyes with a greasy hand. "Kept that wreck of yours operating when it should have been on life support."

Pretending to be insulted, Rick said, "That

wreck of mine hauled your bony butt all over creation, didn't it?''

''Mine and your brothers','' John said on a laugh. Then he sobered up, looked thoughtful and stared off into the distance, past the neatly tended fields, and into the past. ''They were good times, weren't they?''

''The best,'' Rick said softly, though he could barely remember being a teenager whose only worry was where to take his date. Besides, now that he thought about it, he realized that the last few days with Tracy had created more fun memories than most of his teenage years.

A car horn shattered their memories and had both men turning to look at the long road leading up to the farm.

''Well,'' John said with a grin as a familiar car approached, kicking up dust in its wake. ''The gang's all here.''

''Looks like,'' Rick agreed, smiling. He walked toward where the car was already being parked. As two men jumped out before the engine had even finished idling, Rick shouted, "What the hell are you two doing out here?"

Andy Bennet shot a look at his brother Jeff over the roof of their mother's car. "Did you hear that?" he demanded. "Our big brother doesn't seem happy to see us."

"Hell," Jeff retorted, "ain't that just like an officer, though?"

"Yeah," Andy agreed, then remembered that he was an officer in the Corps as well. "Hey!"

"How'd you get mom's car away from her?" Rick asked as he slapped his youngest brother, Andy, on the back.

"Easy," Jeff answered. "We just tied her up and left her in a closet."

"Yeah, right." The day any of her sons could get the best of Patty Bennet was the day the oceans dried up and the sun rose at night.

"She didn't need it," Andy put in, wiggling his thick black eyebrows at his oldest brother. "She was down at the Hall house, planning the wedding you didn't tell us about."

The pretend wedding. Rick scowled slightly, then remembered he was supposed to be the picture of a happy bridegroom and smiled instead. "I don't tell you guys everything."

Jeff shook his head. "I couldn't believe it when Dad told us. Tracy Hall used to be the bane of your life."

"Imagine marrying a girl you called Spot," Andy said.

"I grew up," Rick said stiffly, ready to defend Tracy against even his brothers. "You two ought to try it."

"No, thanks," Jeff said on a laugh. "My second adolescence is too much fun."

Andy suddenly gave a long, low, appreciative whistle as his gaze slid past his brother to the house. There, on the front porch, stood Tracy and Meg, watching the ritual of male bonding.

Rick's heart thudded painfully in his chest and he gave serious thought to killing his little brother when Andy said to no one in particular, ''Looks like Tracy grew up, too. And did a damn fine job of it.''

Forty years' worth of graduates had descended on Juneport and the little town was loving every minute of it. Motels and hotels were packed as reunion weekend loomed closer. The harbor shops did a brisk business as the returnees played tourist, buying up knick-knacks and souvenirs.

Rick bought seal food from the tiny wooden shack at the head of the pier, then handed a bag each to Tracy's nieces and nephews.

The older kids raced off ahead of them, following the distinctive bark and honk of the seals. Four-year-old Jenny, though, kept her hand linked with Rick's, and her brother Tony, a year older, pulled at Tracy, trying to hurry her along.

She laughed and turned to look up at Rick. ''Sorry you volunteered for this mission, Captain?''

The cold ocean wind tossed her hair into a glorious tangle of blond curls and dusted her cheeks with twin spots of rosy color. Her lips curved and her eyes gleamed with pleasure. She was so beautiful it almost hurt to look at her.

Sorry to be with her? Hell, no. He'd only be sorry to leave her when this trip was over.

"It could be risky," she added with a glance at nine-year-old David, who had climbed up on the railing and was now leaning precariously over the edge to improve his view of the seals.

"I'm a Marine," he told her, trying for a light-hearted note. He passed Jenny off to her care before sprinting to the adventurous David's side, "Risk is my business."

Although, he thought, three hours later, he'd rather face an armed enemy than try to ride herd on four excited kids.

"Daunting, aren't they?" Tracy asked and leaned both elbows on the scarred, sun-bleached table.

He glanced at the four kids, now happily immersed in huge bowls of clam chowder. "I don't know how the hell John and Meg do it."

"Stamina," she said, and reached over to wipe Jenny's face.

"You're good with them," Rick said, and knew it was an understatement. She hadn't yelled once all morning. Hadn't lost her temper or her sense of humor.

Tracy looked at the kids before shifting her gaze to his. "It's easy. All it takes is love."

She sure made it look easy, he thought with admiration. They'd walked up and down the harbor. Fed dozens of noisy, smelly seals. Visited every bathroom in a three-block radius. Caught David before he could stow away on a fishing trawler. Bought seven-year-old Becky a new shirt after her brother slapped her with a handful of seaweed. And retraced their steps to find Jenny's missing doll.

Yet Tracy didn't even seem tired. She looked as fresh and gorgeous as she had at the beginning of this long morning.

Love, he told himself. Tracy fairly shone with it. Love streamed from her eyes every time she looked at those kids and they responded in kind. Children, he mused, were smarter than adults. They accepted love as a given and didn't worry about it. No wondering if it was right or wrong. No torturous doubts.

Was he too old to learn from a kid?

"What are you thinking?" she asked, apparently feeling uncomfortable beneath his steady regard.

"I was thinking," he hedged, "just how beautiful you are." He paused, then added, "And how much I'd like to sit on a porch swing with you again sometime."

She was clearly startled, and the wind-kissed color in her cheeks darkened. Eyes wide, she swallowed heavily and shifted in her seat.

At her discomfort, his own grew to monumental proportions. They were both thinking the same thing, he knew. Remembering last night. And wanting it again.

"Rick..."

Whatever she might have said was lost as her oldest nephew made loud kissing noises against the back of his hand.

"That's so gross," David said when he had

their attention. "Soldiers aren't supposed to talk like that. To a *girl*."

Rick swallowed a smile. He'd have to remember to talk to David again in a few years. See if the kid's opinion had changed any.

"I'm pretty, too," Jenny said, tugging on Rick's sleeve until he turned his gaze on her.

Grinning at the dirty little face that watched him so seriously, Rick picked Jenny up and dragged her across his lap. Looking down, he studied her for a long, thoughtful moment before feigning stunned surprise and saying, "You know what?"

"What?"

"You're even *more* beautiful than your Aunt Tracy."

She giggled delightedly and gave him a quick, hard hug. The spontaneous gift of affection speared straight into his heart. The unexpected sweetness of it took his breath away and left him surprisingly defenseless.

His entire adult life, he'd never even considered the possibility of getting married, or having children of his own. Now though, he looked across the table at Tracy.

She smiled at him fondly before his gaze drifted down to her flat, trim abdomen. Even now, his child might be inside this woman. A small, miraculous mixture of him and Tracy.

Just the thought of that both humbled and terrified him. Yet it also had an appeal he hadn't expected to feel.

He lifted his gaze to hers again and he could see by the look on her face that she knew what he'd been thinking. A flicker of worry darted across the depths of her blue eyes and he wished he could reassure her. Wished they could talk about the ''what if'' in both their lives. But now wasn't the time or the place.

Instead, he told himself to be patient. There was still time yet. He smoothed Jenny's tangled hair with a gentle touch and absently wondered if their child would be as sweet and loving as this precious little girl.

Rick didn't see her stick her tongue out at her brother.

He was lost in the realm of possibilities.

Eleven

———

The old gym hadn't stood the test of time well at all.

One of the oldest buildings in town, the school's stone walls looked gray and aged in the afternoon light. Pep squad posters, painted in eye-popping colours, were taped to its walls, giving the place the look of a dignified, elderly matron wearing garishly applied makeup.

But the excited chatter of the reunion committee made the gym echo with memories of the days when the school and its children were young.

Tracy stood near the top of the ladder, trying to stretch her arms far enough to be able to affix the crepe paper streamers to the mint-green wall. "Almost there," she cheered herself from between tightly clenched teeth. "Another inch and..."

"Are you nuts?" A familiar voice from somewhere below her demanded.

Startled, Tracy gasped, released the streamer to flutter to the waxed pine floor and grabbed hold of the top of the ladder with both hands as it swayed beneath her. Only when her heart had left her throat to beat erratically in her chest again did she look down into Rick's outraged green gaze.

"You scared me," she said, in what had to be the understatement of the century.

"You didn't do me any good, either," he said, waving his fingers at her in an attempt to get her to climb down.

He had his Marine face on again, she thought, and she deliberately steeled herself against it. She wasn't one of his subordinates to whom he could issue orders at a whim. As much as she loved him, she wouldn't be pushed around by anybody.

"Hand me the crepe paper," she told him and forced her hands to release their vise-like grip on the ladder.

"Come down and let me do it," he said.

Irritated, she glanced at the handful of people working in the gym. She didn't need more gossip about them than there already was. Thankfully, no one seemed to be paying the slightest attention to them. For the moment. She shifted her gaze back to the man below. "I'm nearly finished."

"Damn straight you are," he said flatly. "You shouldn't be climbing a ladder, for God's sake."

Scowling at him, she lowered her voice to a hissing whisper, "And why shouldn't I?"

He rubbed one hand across his face viciously, glanced around him, then focused on her again. "For one thing, you're already covered in bruises. You're accident prone."

"I am not," she argued, despite the fact that her right hand still ached from where she'd smacked it into the corner of her dresser only that morning.

He pulled himself up two rungs on the ladder and it shook and creaked alarmingly beneath his weight. Tracy's eyes widened and her fingers curled around the aged wood. "Get down," she said quickly. "You'll tip us over."

"It's not just you now, Tracy," he whispered, ignoring her command. "What if you're..." He didn't finish the sentence, just let it hang there.

But then, he didn't need to finish it, did he? She knew exactly what he was talking about. She hadn't even considered it when climbing the ladder. And to be honest, she was still convinced that there was no need for concern. She couldn't be pregnant. Not from her first sexual experience. Even God's sense of humor wouldn't extend that far.

Still. On the off chance...

"Fine. I'll come down," she muttered. Anything was better than continuing this conversation. The longer it went on, the greater the chance of their being overheard.

Rick backed off the ladder and stood at its foot, arms upreached to help her as she neared the bottom. His hands went around her waist and Tracy deliberately suppressed the tell-tale rush of heat that exploded within her at his touch.

"Why didn't you tell me you were helping decorate for the reunion?" he asked, not bothering to loosen his grip on her. "I'd have given you a ride over."

"I thought you were going fishing with your brothers," she said.

Rick smiled and shook his head. The idea of sitting in a cramped boat with his brothers and John had seemed surprisingly unappealing when compared to time spent with Tracy. Of course, when he'd entered the gym and spotted her atop a ladder that was bending like a slender aspen tree in a hurricane, he'd lost ten years of his life. Hadn't he had ample opportunity to note and count every one of the bruises staining her tanned flesh?

He loved her independence. He loved that she leapt right into a situation and gave it everything she had. He just wished she could be a little more careful while she was leaping.

Now, staring down into her blue eyes, he silently asked himself how he expected to get through the rest of his life without being with her every day. He wouldn't be around to see that she took care. He wouldn't be there to assess her injuries. He wouldn't hear her laugh. He wouldn't be there to hold her in the night or to wake up with her in the morning.

All too soon, they'd be heading back to their everyday—separate—lives and this time together would be nothing but a memory. He lifted one hand and smoothed back a single blond curl from her forehead. Could he really make do with just the memory of her to keep him warm?

Is that really what he wanted?

And what choice did he have? Hell, she'd fought against a *pretend* engagement between the two of them. What made him think she'd go for the real thing?

Darkness shimmered close as his future looked long and barren ahead of him.

"Rick?" she prodded, with a tone that told him it wasn't the first time she'd called his name.

Shaking off the blackness still crowding him, he said with a strained laugh, "Fish? When I could be here hanging twisted strips of colored paper instead?"

He released her abruptly. Tracy stepped back, a confused expression on her face. He noticed how empty his hands felt just before he grabbed hold of the ladder and started climbing. "Hand me the streamers, okay?"

She snatched up the joined end of the red and gold crepe paper and held it out to him. Once it was in place, he turned and looked down at her. Tracy gave him a dazzling smile.

"You have a real aptitude for gym decoration."

"Yeah," he said smiling. "On base I'm in huge demand for birthdays and weddings."

That last word seemed to hang in the air between them for a long minute. Until finally,

Tracy cleared her throat and said, "Well, Captain, don't just stand there. We've got a gym to decorate. The reunion's tomorrow. There's no time to waste."

But that's exactly what they were doing, he thought. Wasting precious time. Dancing around their feelings for each other instead of grabbing hold of them and being grateful to whatever gods had gifted them.

"Yes, ma'am," he said and snapped her a salute that set the ladder swaying again.

Tracy laughed and he recorded the sound in his memory.

Tomorrow, the reunion, and after that, his memories would be all he had.

It had seemed like a good idea at the time.

Sixteen of them taking in a movie the night before the reunion. Sixteen adults acting like the kids they used to be, sprawling in the theater seats, throwing popcorn at each other and talking in stage whispers.

Rick frowned to himself and wished he and Tracy were somewhere...*anywhere* else. He wanted privacy. He wanted...hell, he knew what he wanted.

Instead, he thought in disgust, he was sharing her with half the town of Juneport. In the darkness, images flickered on the screen, casting weird shadows of light and dark on the faces of the people in the theater. He didn't have a clue what movie was playing.

Tracy sat next to him, and in the strangely distorted light, he noticed a single tear roll along her cheek. His heart felt as though it was being squeezed in a ham-like fist. Her emotions were so close to the surface. She felt so much. And so deeply.

She blinked, sniffed and when he wrapped his arm around her, she leaned in closer to him, resting her head in the curve of his shoulder. It felt so natural. So right.

And suddenly, it was as if they *were* alone.

He'd meant only to comfort her. But in moments, his hand had strayed from her upper arm to the soft swell of her breast. As if on cue, the action on the screen heated up and

the deafening noise crashing around them
muffled the quiet groan he couldn't quite hide.

Tracy moved closer to him, silently giving
him permission to continue his exploration.

In the darkened theater, his movements
shadowed, Rick slid his hand up to her shoulder and then down, beneath the scooped neck-
line of her pale peach blouse. His teeth
clenched tightly, his fingers slipped across the
top of her lacey bra. She shivered and he felt
her trembling echo inside him.

Past the flimsy barricade separating him
from the flesh he yearned to explore, his nim-
ble fingers found her already erect nipple. He
sucked in a gulp of air as the movie hero laid
his enemies to waste. Tracy shifted in her seat
and cuddled closer, despite the armrest digging into her side.

His fingertips stroked her nipple with feath-
ery touches. She sighed gently, her breath
brushing across the base of his neck. Lower,
deeper, he thrust his hand until he could cup
her fullness in his palm. Gently kneading her

flesh, he tortured them both until his hard, aching groin strained against his jeans.

Swallowing heavily, Rick ignored the movie completely and reached to touch her cheek with his right hand. She turned her face into his palm and kissed it, sliding her tongue across his flesh, leaving a lingering trail of damp warmth.

Around them, the theater darkened further as night crept across the screen.

His thumb and forefinger tweaked and tugged at her nipple. He felt her shiver and shared it when she lifted one hand to cover his, tightening his hold on her breast as if she couldn't bear the thought that he might stop.

Need rushed through him. Hot, hard, relentless. He had to have her. Had to bury his body inside hers. Now.

"Get your coat," he whispered and in the odd light, saw the same, desperate desire that churned within him shining in her eyes.

"Yes," she mumbled, and snatched it from the back of her seat even as he stood up and helped her into the aisle.

The movie audience cheered as Rick, holding Tracy's hand tightly, hurried along the carpeted path toward the doors. Across the brightly lit lobby, through the milling crowd at the snack bar and out into the cold, chill night.

Inside the shelter of his car, they turned to each other and met in a frantic kiss. Tongues tangling, hands touching, breath staggering, they finally broke apart and stared at each other.

"Where can we go?" she whispered in a strangled tone.

"I don't know…" he said and cursed the fact that the small town's motels were booked to the rafters. Desperation inspired an idea that ordinarily he wouldn't have considered. "Okay. Okay."

Firing up the engine, he steered the Range Rover onto the quiet, narrow street. Old-fashioned street lights threw softly muted puddles of yellow across the road. Wisps of fog trailed in from the edge of town, working their way slowly, inexorably toward the heart of Juneport.

''Where?'' Tracy asked, though she didn't really care. She held Rick's right hand in a tight grip, their fingers locked together. Close, she thought. Please, someplace close.

Her heartbeat thundered. The pulse-beat in her throat felt as though it might choke off her air. She'd never known such need. Such desire. Maybe it had been building ever since last night on the porch. She didn't know. All she was sure of was that she had to be with Rick. Had to feel him becoming a part of her again. She needed him more than her next breath.

She wanted another memory of him, because in just a few more days, he would be gone from her life again.

He whipped the car along the familiar streets like a man possessed, as she supposed he was. For both of them, caught in the grip of something so powerful, so unrelenting, there was no escape.

He pulled his hand from hers and reached

instead for her leg. Flipping the hem of her skirt back, he slid his palm along her thigh until he reached the lace-trimmed top of her thigh-high nylons. Rick moaned tightly before skimming his fingertips higher, up to the apex of her thighs.

"Oh, my," she whispered and lifted her hips as high as the confining seatbelt would allow. Holding on to the vinyl padded armrest with a death grip, she let the incredible sensations rocket through her.

"Tracy..." he murmured as his fingertips smoothed over her panty-covered flesh. "I need to touch you."

"I need that, too," she managed to croak. "Hurry, Rick, hurry." She tipped her head back against the head rest and closed her eyes, concentrating on the feel of his hand against her. Already, waves of anticipation surged inside her, building inexorably toward the heart-stopping conclusion she knew was coming.

"Almost there," he said, his hand still toying with the edges of her panties. And then, he was beneath the fragile barrier, touching her skin with delicate strokes that fed her hunger until it was a living thing, crouched inside her, waiting to be released.

He withdrew his hand suddenly and she almost groaned.

Her eyes flew open again as he jerked the car to a stop and threw it into park. Darkness surrounded them. Blacker outlines of tall trees against the night sky towered high, dwarfed only by the silhouette of the old lighthouse. And she knew where they were—beyond the parking area that used to be known as Lover's Point. He'd driven them past the tiny parking lot, across the grass and into the deeper shadows where only the sound of the ocean reached them. It beat and crashed against the rocky shore with a muted, savage roar.

Seatbelts unsnapped, he shifted to her side of the front seat and dragged her across his lap until she straddled his hips, facing him.

''Tracy,'' he muttered her name over and over again as he took her mouth like a man searching for his last breath. His hands lifted the edge of her sweater and pulled it off over her head. He unsnapped her bra, spilling her breasts into his waiting palms. Eagerly, his thumbs edged across her nipples. She arched into him, bracing her hands on his shoulders and rocking her hips against his.

"Can't wait, Tracy," he murmured, tasting first one nipple then the other. "Need you now."

"I need you too, Rick," she said, bracket-ing his face with her hands and tilting his head up until she could look into his eyes. "I need you inside me."

He groaned tightly and released her long enough to free himself from the confining jeans. She twisted and squirmed on his lap to slip out of her panties. Then, he fumbled for his wallet, snatched out a small foil packet and ripped it open.

Tracy looked at the condom, then at him. Smiling, she said breathlessly, "I thought you didn't carry those around anymore."

"Just started recently," he admitted as he sheathed himself.

"I find that very sexy," she whispered and raised herself up on her knees.

"Glad you approve," he said quietly and grasped her hips tightly.

The car windows were fogged over, giving them at least the illusion of being alone in the world. And as he lowered her onto his hard body, he knew he didn't need another soul in his life as long as he had Tracy.

Realization splintered through him. She was everything he could ever want. Everything he would ever need. She was, quite simply, *everything*.

He couldn't let her go. Couldn't go back to the cold, empty world that had become his life. Risk or no risk, he needed Tracy. He wanted to have the kind of marriage his parents had. He wanted kids. He wanted love to be the center of his universe. And for that to happen, he had to have Tracy.

She moved on him, taking him deeper, higher within her. Her head fell back on her neck. He held her and moved her faster, harder. Tracy called out his name as the first tremors coursed through her, and a heartbeat later, he joined her in the crashing climax that left them both breathless.

She lay against him, and Rick's arms closed around her protectively.

"I love you," he murmured, saying aloud for the first time words he'd never thought he'd say.

Instantly, he knew he wasn't going to get the reaction he wanted.

Tracy stiffened slightly and pulled her head back to look at him. "You don't have to say that," she told him.

He frowned at her. "I know I don't *have* to. I wanted to. I love you, Tracy."

Carefully, she disengaged herself from him and shifted slightly so that he could retake his seat behind the steering wheel. As they both moved to readjust their clothing, Tracy went on.

"Don't you think you're taking this fiancé thing a bit far?"

"I'm not pretending, Tracy," he said and reached across the seat to grab one of her hands. "I've been thinking about this for days. In fact, I can't *stop* thinking about it. I don't want to lose you. I want you to marry me. For real."

Tracy gulped in air like a landed fish. For one brief, glorious, radiant moment, she allowed herself to believe. Then reality came raining down on top of her. "You don't love me, Rick," she said, hating the taste of the words on her tongue. "You love the Tracy you've been with all week."

"Yeah," he barked. "You."

"That's not the real me," she said with a slow shake of her head. "I'm not that cool, sleek woman. And you wouldn't want the real me. The woman who rarely wears anything more formal than a sweatshirt and jeans? Who's more comfortable with a good book than with people?"

"Excuse me?" he asked. "I think I know what I feel."

Tracy primly smoothed her skirt down. "I know you think you do," she said.

A hard tap on the window interrupted them and Tracy jumped, startled.

"Damn it," Rick muttered as he rolled down his window. Then he said, "Hello, Mike."

The officer standing outside the car bent low to look inside. Grinning, he glanced from Tracy to Rick. "Aren't you a little old to be parking at the lighthouse, Bennet?"

Rick shot her a quick look before glancing back at his childhood friend. "And gettin' older by the minute," he said.

Straightening up, Officer Mike Destry said, "Do us both a favor, huh? Rent a room."

Tracy covered her face with both hands.

Rick fired up the engine.

"See you guys at the reunion," Mike said and walked back to the squad car parked behind them.

"I can't believe this," Tracy muttered from behind the shield of her cupped hands.

"Look on the bright side," Rick muttered darkly as he watched the police car roll away.

"He could have gotten here five minutes ago."

She groaned loudly. "The whole town will hear about this by tomorrow night."

"Good," Rick said shortly and shoved the gearshift into reverse. "I want the whole damn world to know how I feel about you. Maybe then, you'll believe me."

Twelve

The balloons and streamers looked great. A wildly eclectic selection of music from the last forty years blasted from the speakers placed at either side of the old stage and banners clinging to the walls from drooping tape proclaimed the various graduating classes attending. Tables along both sides of the gym groaned beneath mounds of food provided in a good, old-fashioned pot-luck tradition.

A mob of people crowded the part of the floor set aside for dancing and everything from the fox trot to the indistinguishable current style of dancing was represented.

All in all, it was a terrific party.

So why, Tracy wondered, wasn't she having a good time?

Because, she silently answered her own question, Rick hadn't arrived yet.

Maybe he wasn't coming, she thought. Maybe after last night, he just wanted to stay as far away from her as possible. And maybe, a small voice whispered inside her, that would be best. Even though she longed to see him again, wouldn't it be easier on both of them if they just walked away now?

Her heart twisted painfully at the notion and suddenly the whole reunion and her stupid plan seemed pointless.

Even this dress doesn't matter, she thought, skimming one hand down the sapphire-blue silk creation. She'd bought it to dazzle people she hardly remembered. She'd wanted to make an impression; cast off her cocoon and be the butterfly she'd always dreamed of being. And now the butterfly was trapped in her own net.

Her gaze swept across the entire scene.

Faces blurred, one into the other. Laughter and shouted conversation numbed her ears. Her feet, tortured in a pair of impossibly high heels, were already aching, and the smile she deliberately kept plastered to her face felt as real as the diamond engagement ring on her finger.

It could have been real, she told herself, recalling yet again the proposal Rick had blurted out the night before. She inhaled sharply at the memory, remembering that first, sweet flush of joy she'd experienced before reality had intruded.

Tracy might be new to this whole making love thing, but she knew a passion-induced proposal when she heard one. If he'd been in his right mind, he never would have suggested marriage. How could he?

Someone bumped into her from behind and she whirled around to be met by an unfamiliar, apologetic man. Her gaze dropped to the red-white-and-blue name tag that he, like everyone else in the room, was wearing. *Den-*

nis Thorn. It rang a bell somewhere in the canyons of her memory.

As she thought about it, he glanced at her tag before giving her a stunned look of male appreciation. "Tracy Hall?" he asked, clearly dumbfounded.

"Yes..." she said hesitantly and then placed him. "Dennis. Biology class." Also, her mind whispered, captain of the basketball team, star sprinter and all-around class dreamboat.

"You look fantastic," he said, loud enough to be heard over the music. "I never would have recognized you."

Tracy winced slightly before saying, "Thanks."

Instantly, he realized what his compliment had sounded like. "I didn't mean...well, you know what I meant."

"Yeah." She gave him a practiced smile, said, "I know," and drifted away into the crowd that swallowed her. She knew exactly what he meant. The same thing everyone else she'd talked to that night had meant.

She should be happy, damn it. These were the very reactions she'd hoped to get from her former classmates. And yet, now it didn't seem to matter. Once again, people judged her by her outward appearance. The *real* Tracy, the woman inside, still went unnoticed.

Twisting and turning, she threaded her way through the mass of people, catching snatches of conversation as she passed.

"He's dead, y'know," a man said solemnly.

"Yeah, so's Danny."

"No!"

She moved on quickly.

"Doesn't she look hideous?" The woman sounded appalled.

"What do you expect?" her friend asked. "You use coupons for groceries, not plastic surgery!"

Tracy grimaced tightly and kept moving until she came up behind two women blissfully unaware of her presence.

"So where's the fiancé? That's what *I* want to know."

"You'd think they'd have come together."

Tracy bit her lip. The women were talking about her. She was sure of it. She and Rick were supposed to have driven over to the school together, but she had come early. And had spent every moment since looking for him. Not only a coward, an illogical one at that.

"I knew it was a lie," the woman was saying. "No way would Rick want to marry a little nerd like Tracy Hall...and I don't *care* what she looks like tonight."

Tracy's footsteps faltered, and, despite knowing that eavesdroppers seldom hear anything good about themselves, she cocked an ear to listen masochistically to the rest of the catty woman's speech.

"He's an officer in the Marines, for heaven's sake. He needs a wife with more going for her than an ability to run a computer."

"But..." her friend said.

"After all," the female voice purred, "you can take the nerd out of study hall, but you can't take study hall out of the nerd."

A high-pitched laugh followed this and Tracy hurried on. Blindly, desperately, she needed to get out of this crowd. Everything the woman had said struck far too close to the thoughts that had been running through her own mind since Rick's proposal the night before.

Mumbling apologies, she pushed her way to the closest exit, but before she could escape, a hand on her arm stopped her cold. "Tracy?" a woman asked, "Is that you?"

Steeling herself for another back-handed compliment, Tracy turned to face the woman identified by her name tag as Janelle Taylor, former cheerleader.

"Wow," she was saying. "Meg told me how great you looked, but *wow*."

"Thank you, Janelle," she muttered. "You, too."

The other woman laughed and gave her ample hips a pat. "Thanks, but three kids have ended my bathing-beauty days."

"Three? Congratulations," Tracy said, with her first genuine smile all evening.

"Don't encourage me," Janelle warned her. "At the slightest provocation I can produce mountains of pictures."

Two or three other women sidled closer as Janelle went on. "Meg tells me you have your own business now. Computers, isn't it?"

"That's right," Tracy said giving the other women a cautious look.

"Isn't that great?" one of them murmured. "I'd love to work for myself."

"So," Janelle asked, "do you design your own programs or what?"

Surprised, Tracy looked from one to the other of the women and realized that they were actually interested. In her. Not her engagement. Not her new look. *Her.*

She relaxed a bit and named one of her latest designs, at which point one of her listeners squealed.

"That was *your* work?" she said, grabbing Tracy's hand. "That program saved my husband's company thousands of dollars!" She turned to look over the crowd. "Wait'll I tell him who you are...."

Tracy shook her head. "He wouldn't know my name. I'm just another computer nerd."

"Yeah," the woman said on a wry laugh. "So's Bill Gates."

Well. She'd never thought of it like *that* before.

"Imagine," someone else muttered just loud enough for Tracy to hear, "she's gorgeous, has a great career *and* Rick Bennet. Life doesn't get much more perfect than that."

A small, wistful smile crossed her face briefly. Her life wasn't perfect. No one's was. But, she'd never realized before just how good her life really was.

The fake engagement—Brad—seemed so silly now. She didn't need a man to make her feel successful. She'd built a bustling business from scratch. She had a nice house. A few good friends. A family who loved her. What more could a woman want?

Rick, a voice inside whispered.

But she told herself firmly, even without Rick, her life would be pretty darn good.

Just, she thought with a pang, substantially lonelier.

Rick came up behind her in time to hear the tail end of the conversation. He'd been trying to get to Tracy for the last hour, but had been stopped by half of his graduating class along the way. A man in a dress blues uniform always commanded attention.

He caught Janelle's eye, and she gave him a slow once-over before grinning at him. "Tracy," she said, "I think this guy wants a dance."

She turned around to face him and for Rick, everyone else in the room faded away. The blue of her dress was reflected in her eyes and the diamond drops hanging from her ears glittered and shone in the overhead lights. She'd been avoiding him since last night and now that he had her right in front of him, she'd struck him speechless.

A long moment passed before he got himself under control enough to say simply, "Dance with me, Tracy."

She nodded and when he took her hand in

his, she followed him to the dance floor. A ballad from the sixties swelled from the speakers. He pulled her into his arms and swayed in time to the music.

"We were supposed to attend this thing together," he said. "Why did you come without me?"

"I thought it would be easier," she said, keeping her gaze lowered.

"For you?"

"For both of us," she said.

"You look beautiful," he whispered in her ear and inhaled her soft, flowery fragrance.

"Thank you."

"I love you," he said.

Her gaze snapped up to his. Regret shimmered in her eyes and he felt a tight fist squeeze his heart. "Don't, Rick. Please don't."

"I want to marry you, Tracy."

All around them, couples swirled and talked, lost in their own worlds and oblivious to everyone else.

"There's no need," she said, her words a

hush of sound meant for him alone. "I told you, the chances of me being—you know—are microscopically slim."

"That's not what this is about," he argued. Sure, if she was pregnant with his child, he wanted to be a part of it. But more than that, he wanted to be a part of Tracy's life. Tracy's heart. He hadn't expected to fall so hopelessly in love, but damn it, now that he had, she could at least believe him.

She tried to pull away from him, but he held her close, somehow terrified that if he let her go now, she'd be lost to him forever. And in the last few days, he'd discovered that his life was empty without her in it. In the military or out, marriage was a risky proposition. But damn it, some risks were worth taking.

If only, he thought, tightening his hold on her, he could convince her to risk her heart on him.

"I love you, Tracy," he said again, his voice pitched so only she would hear.

She shook her head and he thought he

caught a glimmer of unshed tears in her eyes. "No. You don't."

Stubborn. Hardheaded. His grip on her waist tightened, pulling her even closer against him.

The music stopped abruptly, startling the dancers, and a middle-aged man strolled across the stage to take the microphone. Again, Tracy tried to slip away, but Rick couldn't let her go. Not now. Not ever.

"Okay, folks," the man on stage announced gleefully, "it's time to make the presentations. Everybody here got to vote on these prizes and now we see who gets what."

Applause and laughter rose up from the crowd as the people surged closer, packing more tightly together. Tracy was shoved up against Rick and he wrapped both arms around her for good measure. He wasn't going to give up. Not when his—their—whole future was at stake.

When this ceremony was over, he'd take her outside. Where they could talk. Somehow, he'd find the words to convince her of his love. He'd make her believe.

The next few minutes passed quickly as small trophies were handed out to the oldest attendee and the youngest, the person who travelled farthest and several other awards. At last, the announcer said, ''Now our trophy for the most changed Juneport graduate.'' He paused for effect, checked the paper in his hand, then looked out over the crowd and said, ''Tracy Hall.''

She stiffened slightly in Rick's arms and nodded to the people near them who offered congratulations. Polite applause rippled in the air as Rick reluctantly released her. Quietly, she made her way to the stage and climbed the steps to receive her award.

Every eye in the place was on her. Tracy's stomach jumped nervously as she took the tiny trophy and held it in both trembling hands. And then it was her turn to make a short speech.

Clutching the silly award tightly, she looked out over the crowd, noting the familiar faces…her parents, sister, Rick's family. And finally, Rick. He looked impossibly handsome in his Marine dress uniform. Tall and proud and so damned good. Then he smiled at her and Tracy realized what it was she had to say.

She cleared her throat and hoped her voice wouldn't be choked off by the sudden swell of emotion rising within her. "Thank you," she said, letting her gaze slide across the listening crowd, "but I don't think I really deserve this."

Confused muttering drifted toward her, but she kept right on talking.

"You see, I haven't changed. Not really." Shaking her head, she waved one hand in front of her to encompass her appearance. "Under this pretty dress and the makeup, I'm still me. Tracy the Nerd." She took a breath and said, "It's you who've changed. All of you. I guess it's growing up. We stop classifying people and try to look at each other as individuals."

The muttering grew a bit louder, but Tracy wasn't finished. "I…wanted to come home *different.* The new and improved Tracy Hall.'' A rueful chuckle escaped her. ''But I finally discovered that the *old* Tracy is good enough for me.''

A smattering of applause and she smiled at her mom and dad. Then she shifted her gaze back to Rick's and finished her little confession. ''As long as I'm being honest here, you should know that I'm not engaged, either.'' Briefly, she glanced away from Rick's scowling face to look at her family. ''See, I wanted to impress all of you, so I made up a fiancé and then Rick volunteered for the job...and, well...things just got out of hand, I guess.'' The edges of the trophy dug into her palms as she ended her speech.

Strained silence greeted her and Tracy bit down hard on the inside of her cheek. Confession might be good for the soul, she thought. But it was hard on her heart. Hers ached for the ending of her little fantasy.

Then she heard it. One pair of hands slapping together. Soft clapping that slowly rose in strength and volume. Turning her head, she looked at Rick as he walked toward the stage, continuing his solitary ovation.

The people in front of him parted, clearing a path for him and she could almost hear them all wondering what was going to happen next. So was she.

When he was directly in front of the stage, standing just below her, he stopped, looked at her and said in a loud, clear voice, "Marry me, Tracy."

"Rick..." she looked away from him long enough to note the blossoming smiles on the interested crowd's faces.

"Marry me," he repeated, louder this time. "I love you."

Why was he doing this? Her gaze locked with his, she saw stubborn determination gleaming in his green eyes and Tracy knew there was no way to avoid this.

"You don't even know me, Rick," she said, resigned now to a very public conversation. "You can't possibly love me."

"You're wrong," he said flatly.

She shook her head and felt the sting of

tears. Her grip on the trophy tightened like a drowning man's on a liferope.

Slowly, Rick smiled at her and her heartbeat staggered.

Then he started talking as if they were alone and not surrounded by half the town. "I love the way you notice waiters' name tags and address them like they're old friends."

Tracy's breath hitched.

"I love your gentleness with kids. I love that you have as much fun as they do." He shook his head slightly. "I love the way you help me see the beauty in a sunset. Your laughter warms me and your tears break my heart."

Tracy pulled in a long, shuddering breath.

Rick grinned. "I love that you put ice cubes in your soup to cool it off before you eat it."

Someone in the crowd laughed.

A tear rolled down Tracy's cheek.

"I love that you wear your glasses because your contacts hurt."

Breathe, Tracy, she reminded herself. Breathe.

"And I love that your idea of a good book is a technical manual."

More laughter and this time, even Tracy smiled. Something warm and wonderful settled in the pit of her stomach as she looked down into the face of the man she loved so completely.

He hadn't just noticed her carefully cultivated appearance. He'd really seen *her*. He loved *her*.

"You do know me," she said softly, her voice breaking.

"Mostly, though," he continued, his gaze moving over her face with a tender thoroughness, "I like who I am when I'm with you. I love that we are...together. I love you, Tracy." Smiling, he added, "And you love me." Reaching for her hand, he removed the ring she'd bought for herself and quickly replaced it with the one he'd purchased just that afternoon. The white gold band held a star sapphire surrounded by diamonds.

"The sapphire reminded me of your eyes," he said, then planted a kiss on her ring finger.

"Oh, Rick..." she whispered, her gaze flashing from the ring to his face.

The whole room seemed to take a collective breath as the gathered crowd waited expectantly.

But she was hardly aware of them. Her gaze locked with Rick's, she found her future written in his eyes and silently thanked whatever fates had led her to this one, magical moment. Quietly, she said the words she knew he was waiting for. "I do."

He lifted a warning finger. "Remember that phrase."

More muffled chuckling from their audience.

Tracy grinned and nodded. In one short week, she'd found the love of her life. What had started as an impossible plan for ridiculous reasons had become the beginning of an entirely new life. One to be shared and cherished. Looking into his deep, green eyes, she said softly, "Who needs Brad, anyway?"

Rick laughed and held up his arms. She leaned into him and he swung her down from the stage and into a long, slow, deep kiss that had the women closest to them sighing in heartfelt envy.

Thunderous applause shook the room.

And as Tracy wrapped her arms around his neck and gave herself up to the magic that lay between them, she thought she heard someone nearby whisper, ''Who's Brad?''

Epilogue

——

Camp Pendleton, base hospital
Eight months and three weeks later

"Come on Tracy," the doctor urged, "one more good push."

"I can't," she said on a groan and sank back, exhausted, into her husband's arms. "Too tired."

"You can do this, Trace," Rick murmured, smoothing her sweat-soaked hair back from her forehead. "You *have* to do this," he added with a soft smile.

"No, I don't," she countered weakly. "I quit."

He laughed and shook his head. "You can't quit now, honey. The baby's almost here."

Nobody knew that better than Tracy. Already, deep within her, the next pain lay curled up, awaiting the strength to announce itself.

Tracy pulled in a deep breath, reached up to touch Rick's cheek and said, "Take me home, okay?"

He kissed her palm and shook his head. "Can't, honey. Not until you've finished here."

"I changed my mind," she said, shifting her gaze to the doctor sitting on a stool at the foot of the bed. "I want a C-section. Or an epidural. Or a hammer over the head."

"Too late," the doctor told her gently. "Your baby's almost born, Tracy."

"See, honey," Rick said, planting a quick kiss on her forehead. "One more push and we'll have that baby we've been waiting for."

"Too tired," she muttered. After ten long

hours of hard labor, all she wanted to do was sleep.

"You can do this, Trace," Rick said again.

The pain blossomed, reaching for her, spreading its tentacles out to every corner of her body. She groaned at its build-up, knowing darn well what was coming.

"I can't."

"You can." Rick saw the fatigue in her eyes, and shared it. After watching the woman he loved suffer all night, all he wanted to do was snatch her up off the bed and run away. Protect her. Care for her. But now wasn't the time for sympathy. As a trained Marine, he knew that sometimes what his troops needed was a good swift kick. Metaphorically speaking, of course.

Lowering his voice, he whispered in her ear, "Remember when I told you that we'd made a baby that first night in the motel?"

She nodded.

"I was right, wasn't I?"

She gave him a wry smile. "I don't think you'll ever let me forget it."

Darn right. A husband had to hang on to every advantage he could get. "Well, I'm right about this, too. Come on, honey, one more push and we're outta here."

"You promise?"

Unwilling to promise what he couldn't guarantee, Rick looked to the doctor first. At the man's nod, he turned back to his wife. "I promise."

"Okay..." she said, already grimacing as the pain claimed her.

He lifted her up, bracing her in his strong arms.

Taking a deep breath, she moaned a little, then closed her eyes and pushed for all the marbles.

An eternity later, the doctor yelled, "Way to go Tracy, that's it!"

A baby's indignant wail sliced through the air and a couple of the nurses laughed delightedly.

Rick simply stared at the small, squirming, red-fleshed infant they'd waited for for so long. He felt Tracy's hand grab his and he looked at her as tears coursed freely down his face.

"She's so beautiful," Tracy crooned as the doctor handed her her daughter.

Rick leaned over his family, stroked a fingertip along his little girl's cheek and grinned. "She's not only beautiful," he said firmly. "She's the next generation of Bennet Marines."

"I love you, Captain."

"I love you too, Spot."

* * * * *

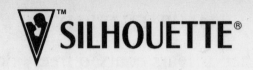

SILHOUETTE®

LARGE PRINT TITLES FOR
JULY – DECEMBER 2002

SPECIAL EDITION™

July:	DADDY BY DEFAULT	Muriel Jensen
August:	BETH AND THE BACHELOR	Susan Mallery
September:	DADDY BY DESIGN	Muriel Jensen
October:	THE IRRESISTIBLE MR SINCLAIR	Joan Elliott Pickart
November:	DADDY BY DESTINY	Muriel Jensen
December:	HUNTER'S WOMAN	Lindsay McKenna

DESIRE™

July:	HIS WOMAN, HIS CHILD	Beverly Barton
August:	MUM IN WAITING	Maureen Child
September:	HAVING HIS BABY	Beverly Barton
October:	BLACKHAWK'S SWEET REVENGE	Barbara McCauley
November:	LEAN, MEAN AND LONESOME	Annette Broadrick
December:	SECRET BABY SANTOS	Barbara McCauley

SENSATION™

July:	A HERO FOR ALL SEASONS	Marie Ferrarella
August:	WHEN YOU CALL MY NAME	Sharon Sala
September:	WHAT THE BABY KNEW	Ingrid Weaver
October:	A FOREVER KIND OF HERO	Marie Ferrarella
November:	THE ADMIRAL'S BRIDE	Susanne Brockmann
December:	EMILY AND THE STRANGER	Beverly Barton